D1130694

Return to Dar al-Basha

Middle East Literature in Translation
Michael Beard *and* Adnan Haydar, *Series Editors*

Other titles in Middle East Literature in Translation

Return to
Dar al-Basha

A NOVEL

◆ ◆ ◆

Hassan Nasr

Translated from the Arabic by
William Hutchins

SYRACUSE UNIVERSITY PRESS

Copyright © 2006 by Syracuse University Press
Syracuse, New York 13244–5160
All Rights Reserved

First Edition 2006
06   07   08   09   10   11   6   5   4   3   2   1

Originally published in Arabic as *Dar al-Basha* by Hasan Nasr (Tunis: Dar al-Janub li-l-Nashr, 1994, 1998).

Permission to publish English translations from *Nahr al-Ramad* by Khalil Hawi as granted by his brother Dr. Sami Hawi is gratefully acknowledged.

Chapter 17 has appeared in a slightly different translation in *Banipal,* no. 26 (Summer 2006).

The paper used in this publication meets the minimum requirements of American National Standard for Information Sciences—Permanence of Paper for Printed Library Materials, ANSI Z39.48–1984.∞™

Library of Congress Cataloging-in-Publication Data
Naṣr, Ḥasan, 1937–
[Dār al-Bāshā. English]
Return to Dar al-Basha : a novel / Hassan Nasr ; translated from the Arabic by William Hutchins.—1st ed.
p. cm.—(Middle East literature in translation)
Translated from Arabic.
Includes bibliographical references.
ISBN 0–8156–0878–0 (hardcover : alk. paper)
I. Hutchins, William M. II. Title.
PJ7852.A685D3713 2006
892.7'36—dc22
2006024604

Manufactured in the United States of America

♦　　♦　　♦

"You, flying there . . .
Answer me, my life for yours:
What is it?
Are you wounded?
Is there something you seek?"
"No, it's art and art's melancholy,
For an artist knows many cares and sorrows."
He deemed himself responsible for all existence, as if
    existence had no master of its own.
"Free yourself from the burdens of life and let's be off
With faces as cheerful as the morning's.
It's presumptuous to attempt to bear the world's burdens,
Since their weight is too great for you even to budge.
Mighty existence has sunk low in the past,
But you're not its lord to set it right."

                    —Abu al-Qasim al-Shabbi
                      Aghani al-Hayat (Songs of Life)

♦ ♦ ♦

Leave me alone! In my eyes,

The lighthouses of the way have gone dark.

Let me proceed into the unknown.

Distant harbors will never tempt me:

Neither those [Western ones] of feverish clay,

Nor those [Eastern ones] of lifeless clay.

Oh! How I've been scorched by the feverish clay!

Oh! How I've been asphyxiated by the lifeless clay!

Distant harbors will never tempt me.

Leave me to the sea, to the wind, to death,

Where shrouds are spread in blue for the drowning man,

The seafarer, in whose eyes the lighthouses of the way

have gone dark;

Their light has died in his eyes. It is dead.

No act of heroism can save him, not even servile prayer.

—Khalil Hawi
"The Mariner and the Dervish,"
from *Nahr al-Ramad*

Contents

Hassan Nasr was born in Tunis, on February 4, 1937. He studied at ez-Zitouna Mosque in Tunis and then in Baghdad at the College of Literary Arts. He has taught in Tunisia and in Mauritania. Among contemporary Arab novelists, he is unusually well versed in traditional Islamic studies. His publications, which include short story collections and novels, display an innovative use of Islamic cultural references and a passionate social conscience.

William Maynard Hutchins, who teaches at Appalachian State University of North Carolina, was the principal translator of *The Cairo Trilogy* by Naguib Mahfouz. A recipient of a 2005–2006 grant for literary translation from the National Endowment for the Arts, he has published several volumes of translations from Arabic literature and *Tawfiq al-Hakim: A Reader's Guide*.

Acknowledgments

I wish to thank the author for entrusting his important novel to us; my friend of many years and excellent collaborator Béchir Chourou for contacting Hassan Nasr and for correcting many of the chapters; my friends Imad and Abdelaziz Houimdi of Angers, France, for their assistance; M. and Mme. Béchir Melliti, also of Angers, for their help with some obscure vocabulary; Roger Allen for suggesting this novel; the readers and editors from Syracuse University Press for their suggestions and editing; T. Marvin Williamsen, Robert White, and the Angers Committee of Appalachian State University for sponsoring my year in France, where this translation was prepared; and Sarah, Franya, and Kip Hutchins for their complaisance. All notes were prepared for this translation.

Introduction

$\mathcal{R}$*eturn to Dar al-Basha*, which takes its name from a neighborhood in the medina or old city of Tunis, intro-duces us to a man so traumatized by childhood mistreat-ment that he has never recovered. The reader meets the main character, Murtada al-Shamikh, as he returns home after an absence of forty years, determined to make peace with his past. As he penetrates deeper into the old city he remembers vivid scenes from his childhood and youth. In the courtyard of his family's home, he encounters a tor-toise—a soft, timid creature hiding inside a hard shell— and this is a fitting image for the scared boy hiding inside the embittered man.[1]

Hassan Nasr excels as a miniaturist, and many of his publications have been collections of short stories. Even his novels—with the possible exception of *Dahaliz al-Layl* (Night Passages, 1977)—consist of a sequence of polished vignettes. In an early collection, *Layali al-Matar* (Rainy Nights, 1967), for example, the stories typically present a

1. Image courtesy of Kip G. Hutchins.

complex emotion that the protagonist (who may be the narrator) experiences as the result of chance encounters. Even *Dahaliz al-Layl,* which is a plotted narrative that ends with a climax involving three related deaths, arguably was designed to display the protagonist's psychological state at the time of the climax. Given the context provided by Hassan Nasr's other works, *Return to Dar al-Basha* can be understood as a series of encounters, each of which evokes a remembered scene and all of which form a chain of events that culminate in the earthquake nightmare sequence, during which Murtada experiences complex psychological turmoil.

Some stylistic characteristics that are found throughout Hassan Nasr's works include changes of person in the narration, Qur'anic citations, Sufi references, terse exposition, use of an epigraph to set a work's tone, an existentialist flavor, comments on the role of the arts in society, and an embrace of melancholy.

The narration in a novel or short story by Hassan Nasr may shift person from third to first or second person without warning. In *Return to Dar al-Basha,* all three persons are used, but each normally refers to the hero Murtada; thus the shift should not confuse a reader. We all know someone who begins: "I have a friend with a problem . . ." even though we understand he is speaking about himself. Murtada, the protagonist, and the narrator converge into a single person who talks about himself in both the first and third persons as well as to himself in the second person. In this novel, the shifting perspective does not suggest a character with a multiple personality or shifts of perspective by the character. It is, rather, comparable to the multiple perspectives of a Cubist painting. By shifting between different persons, the author turns the narration into a dialogue the hero is having with himself and therefore also with the reader, who becomes complicit. The frequent Qur'anic citations—in this novel as in daily life—create an unobtrusive extra voice in Arabic. Similarly, the novel's sections are named after the portions into which the Qur'an is divided for reading.

Return to Dar al-Basha has not just one epigraph but two, and these are paired as a dialogue. Ideally they should appear as a centerfold diptych inscribed in excellent calligraphy on handmade paper. The poem of Abu al-Qasim al-Shabbi seems to answer the Lebanese poet Khalil Hawi's "The Mariner and the Dervish," which celebrates a seafarer who drowns in solitude so definitive that: "No act of heroism can save him, not even servile prayer."[2] The Tunisian poet al-Shabbi, by contrast, comforts and chastises a melancholy poet for deeming himself: "responsible for all existence, as if existence had no master of its own."[3] The upbeat ending of *Return to Dar al-Basha* may result from Murtada's realization that he is not responsible for his whole neighborhood, let alone the whole world. This surmise may be faulty, however, since the comforting poem is printed before the melancholy one.

In addition to these two poems, a citation from the

2. Khalil Hawi, "The Mariner and the Dervish," in his *Nahr al-Ramad* (River of Ashes), 3rd printing (Beirut: Dar al-Tali'a li-l-Tiba'a wa-l-Nashr, 1963), 19.

3. Abu al-Qasim al-Shabbi, *Aghani al-Hayat* (Songs of Life) (Tunis: al-Dar al-Tunisiya li-l-Nashr, 1966).

fourteenth-century Tunisian historian Ibn Khaldun, functions as an embedded epigraph, for it occupies a conspicuous point in a long internal dialogue. The quotation from Ibn Khaldun emphasizes the evolution and decline of individuals, eras, and cities—in other words—the constant flux that shapes human life on both individual and collective levels.

The contrast between Murtada's placid reunion with his family and his nightmare generates for the reader a dialogue comparable to that of some other North African voices. In *The Colonizer and the Colonized*, for example, Tunisian-born Albert Memmi writes, "The revolt of the adolescent colonized, far from resolving into mobility and social progress, can only sink into the morass of colonized society—unless there is a total revolution."[4] Frantz Fanon, the French Caribbean psychiatrist who sided with the Algerian revolution, said both: "Decolonization is the veritable creation of new men," and, "If the last shall be first, this will only come to pass after a murderous and decisive struggle between the two protagonists."[5]

The implied comparison between the father's brutal paternalism and the abuses of colonial rule is a typical theme in twentieth-century Arab literature. In *Return to Dar al-Basha* liberation comes via an interior struggle. Murtada ran away from home years ago but never escaped from his father's shadow. He frees himself only when he

4. Albert Memmi, *The Colonizer and the Colonized* (New York: Orion, 1965), 99.

5. Frantz Fanon, *The Wretched of the Earth*, trans. Constance Farrington (New York: Grove Press, 1966), 30.

embarks on a nightmare version of Descartes's first "Meditation" and, like Descartes, attempts to determine what he knows for certain, starting as a self in a void. Just as Descartes began by pretending total skepticism only to conclude his six meditations with a conviction of almost total certainty, Murtada acknowledges that the traditional, patriarchal culture facilitated the abuse he suffered as a child, but realizes that the culture was also a vibrant one. His feelings are complicated by the fact that this culture was also coming apart at the seams under colonial pressure, which patriots like Murtada's uncle Mansur resisted.

In an introduction to *Modern Japanese Aesthetics*, Michele Marra discusses the use by Meiji-era Japanese critics of imported Western aesthetics to forge a modern Japanese national identity: "All the authors are moved by an impulse to define Japan to themselves in an attempt at clarifying their own subjectivities to themselves."[6] In *Return to Dar al-Basha*, Hassan Nasr defines the protagonist's subjectivity and thus clarifies the Tunisian identity. The French scholar Jean Fontaine, who has lived for years in Tunisia, has thus said that Murtada's search for his identity is representative of the search by Tunisians in general for their own.[7] According to Frantz Fanon, the subjective alienation that a colonized person feels is not an idiosyncratic personal quirk: "The oppressor . . . manages to im-

6. Michele Marra, *Modern Japanese Aesthetics: A Reader* (Honolulu: University of Hawaii Press, 1999), 7.

7. Jean Fontaine, *Le Roman tunisien de langue arabe: 1956–2001* (Tunis: Cérès Editions, 2002), 108.

pose on the native new ways of seeing, and in particular a pejorative judgement with respect to his original forms of existing."[8] The typical, wistful, melancholy, alienated, idiosyncratic protagonist of *Return to Dar al-Basha*—and of many other works by Hassan Nasr—is then, arguably, representative of colonized and neo-colonized peoples of the twentieth century.

William Hutchins

8. Frantz Fanon, *Toward the African Revolution*, trans. Haakon Chevalier (New York: Grove Press, 1967), 38.

Preamble

◆　　◆　　◆

The World of Colors

1

*P*asha Street slips through the mazes of the old city of Tunis, penetrating its inner recesses and extending a long arm west to Bab al-Banat and eastward to Ramadan Bey Square, from which it proceeds to Qasr al-Qasaba and ez-Zitouna Mosque. It is the shortest route from the city's neighborhoods to its heart, which throbs with souks and motion.

As you enter the Dar al-Basha neighborhood, you discover the special aroma it derives from perfumes that waft in every direction and from the pungent, heady spices that fill the air wherever you turn. As you advance down its covered streets and narrow passageways you linger, contemplating spaces washed by rainbow colors and the soft light that steals through gaps between the fingers of the district's hands: peeking from the eyes of windows that overlook the street on each side, slipping through the cracks of doors left ajar and over rooftops.

You move beneath low arches with decorated vaults, through domed passageways, past columns topped with capitals and portals radiant with lines, ornamentation, and color. Life in all its splendor pours into buildings set at angles to the street, through doors facing each other and protruding grills of windows that look down on the road like lofty, green candelabra fastened to walls smeared with sunlight. Large, high doors are decorated with projecting black bolt-heads and iron circles that dangle like earrings over round domes: audacious, nude breasts on virgins' chests.

Here's Murtada al-Shamikh returning with a new heart to Dar al-Basha, inhaling the neighborhood's familiar atmosphere, after a lengthy absence of forty years or more. He pauses, scrutinizing places that seared him and drove him away, places where he once lived. Assorted echoes from the past reverberate deep inside him as people, voices, events, buildings, and familiar songs spill from his heart.

He plunges deep into areas where he will open doors to reveal his past so that he can turn its pages and reread it. He obviously committed some offense early in life. He must search out this error, because that misstep has molded his life ever since, pursuing him wherever he has gone through the passing years. He has attached many names to that error. He would call it a curse that pursued him. He would term it vexing bad luck. Then again he would think it an affliction that had beset him.

We all learned in arithmetic that a minor error in a preliminary but critical operation inevitably leads to an erroneous conclusion, even if we follow correct procedures in solving the problem. An initial error inevitably entails a subsequent one.

The sense of failure haunting him through all the

stages of his life must have had some cause. It certainly originated with that first error he had never attempted to rectify, believing that it was so far removed he could not circle back to it and that distance and the passage of time would eventually erase it. Instead, distance and time had only rendered it more dreadful and oppressive. Similarly, when you wear shoes that are too small for your feet, you have difficulty walking and your feet hurt, until you replace them with shoes the right size.

As Murtada al-Shamikh proceeded through the Dar al-Basha neighborhood, he told himself, "This is the bridge you must cross from the past to the present, from exile to exile. You came here unwillingly and left in flight. You return once more to search for meaning. Take your time here if you can. Except when you're pressed, let the pieces fall where they will, for you 'shall never cleave the earth to its core or rival the mountains in height.' "[1]

---

1. Qur'an 17:37 (Banu Isra'il, meaning "the Children of Israel"). The context is a set of divine instructions for human life, and the "you" refers to all of us generic human beings.

2

$\mathcal{G}$rasping his hand, she hurried through the Halfaouine neighborhood to Bab Souïka. From there she dragged him into the souks of the old city, through swelling crowds, past clamorous vendors, kaleidoscopic hues, and variegated displays and finery. Surrendering himself to that world of colors, people, and objects, the boy forgot the anxiety that had tormented him and relaxed his small hand, which had started to ache in the woman's firm grip.

She herded him into the shrine of Sidi Mahrez and along its vast, commodious gallery, which was a place of refuge for the bewildered, the troubled, and the afflicted. A strange scene confronted him. Children wailed loudly while women moved about like wraiths or sat by the gallery's wall, their gazing stares blank, their garments threadbare. A rubbish heap lay next to piles of miscellaneous items, badly worn mats, and soiled carpeting. Dishes were strewn about, and the floor was awash with refuse and liquid wastes. Nearby, a child urinated. Filth was neighbor to screams, sores and swellings to weeping. One crone leaned against the wall, and another hobbled along with a crooked stick. A mother called to her daughter Sa'diya, while another offered a breast to her infant. From a different direction, voices were raised in a heated dispute between several women. Waving their arms to deliver curses and oaths, their hair disheveled, they flung choice insults at each other as saliva sprayed from their mouths.

She guided him down the long gallery, and they entered, by its large portal, the sanctuary of the holy saint Sidi Mahrez. The splendid chamber was paved with white marble, and its walls, covered with colored tiles, rose to disappear in a vast expanse of space beneath the broad, lofty dome. She headed for a well in a corner of the hall. A woman stationed there provided water to visitors. Aunt Munjiya drew the veil from her face, revealing a forehead dripping with sweat. She pulled her sleeves back from her forearms, took the bucket by its strap, and leaned over the white marble basin. She started pouring cold water over her face and hands to drown the summer heat. She filled a clay jug with the water and handed this to the boy so he could drink. She drank after him and then extracted from the folds of her voluminous bosom a handkerchief to dry her face and hands. Next, she proceeded to the holy saint's sepulcher. Removing her shoes at the door, she entered on tiptoe, cautiously and timorously, the boy trailing after her. This large chamber's walls were covered all the way to the ceiling with tiles that sported green crescent moons in radiant orange squares on a light background. An oval ceiling rested on symmetrical crystal arches through which light spilled, flooding the chamber's expanse.

On one side of the room stood a white cage of dazzlingly beautiful iron grillwork with the tomb at its center. A bright green wooden barrier encircled the cage. Mumbling her prayers, Aunt Munjiya stood before the tomb, where a row of candles burned and sticks of incense released vapors of a pungent and pervasive fragrance. Women brought votive offerings. Scraps of cloth of every color were tied to the tomb's grill. There were flags and banners of many hues, rows of prayer books, copies of the Qur'an spread out next to each other, small carpets unfurled, and lamps. A multi-tiered chandelier was suspended from the top of the domed ceiling, and the walls were hung with panels inscribed, in gold leaf, with God's exceptionally beautiful names. There were charms, heady perfumes, verses from the Holy Qur'an and other inscriptions.

Weary women worshipers had been arriving since dawn. They sought respite for their souls amid the green columns under the towering ceiling, releasing heartfelt wishes in prayer. Some grasped the bars of the tomb's grill or leaned against the wooden barrier. Others were engrossed in prayer.

The boy watched a kneeling woman forcefully grasp the bars of the grill. Tears flowed down her cheeks as she directed her pleas toward the saint's resting place: "Sidi Mahrez, my love, my saint, I have come to you, my master, to lament my condition. Relieve my distress and place me under your protection. Give the unjust tyrant his richly deserved punishment and ensure that my rights prevail, for I am an oppressed orphan, and you are my master and guardian."

The boy listened, watching her in astonishment.

Through his mind's eye passed the scene of his mother and her sister Dalila in a corner of the house's courtyard, when they had stood near the door of the hall, beneath the gutter, as their paternal uncle, his outer cloak flapping, slapped their faces while they wept and wailed. He felt sorry for this woman, approached her, and tugged at the hem of her robe, either to get a closer look or to pat her dress to console her. She did not notice him. Her tears flowed copiously, and she was oblivious to him and everything else around her. She sensed nothing and observed nothing.

Aunt Munjiya recited the preamble of the Qur'an and left stealthily, on tiptoe, just as she had entered. After slipping on her shoes, she took his hand again, and they retraced their steps up the long, crowded gallery.

Ever since she had taken him from his mother and left the house, he had trailed behind her, silently and apprehensively. For the first time he roused himself from his daze and broke his silence to ask, "Where are we going?"

"To the wedding house, like your mother said. Do you doubt it? Step lively and don't ask too many questions."

She continued through the Sidi Mahrez souk, dragging him through its crowds. While her attention was caught by a display, a man accosted her from behind: "Where are you going, woman? I've seen you making the rounds of the market."

She turned nervously. "Who's that? Salih al-Fayyash, where did you spring from?"

He took her aside, and they began to talk. This Salih al-Fayyash was of compact build and had large black eyes with bushy eyebrows. His mustache was narrow and black, and he wore his long *jebba*,[1] which had red and black stripes, brazenly over a shoulder and across his chest. He began to study the boy with wide eyes. Then, stretching out a hand, he tousled the boy's hair. "So, this is Abd al-Jabbar's son."

At that moment, Aunt Munjiya moved to block the boy from hearing their conversation. As she turned again and momentarily merged with the market crowd, her voice was lost in the general confusion. Salih al-Fayyash purchased a piece of sesame-seed candy. He offered it to the boy, toward whom he became increasingly affectionate: "Here you go, Murtada. Your name's Murtada, isn't it? Won't you take this?"

When Murtada refused the candy, Aunt Munjiya poked him between the shoulders to force him to accept it: "Take it. It's wrong for kids to refuse something a grown man offers."

He presented the candy to the boy, kissed his forehead, and instructed her to take good care of the lad. Then he bade her goodbye and vanished into the crowd.

Although the boy accepted the candy, he held it without tasting it. He was feeling glum and had no interest in food or drink. He was suspicious of these goings-on and feared that some treachery was afoot. He sensed all this from the woman's tone. His anxiety was heightened also by the way she had moved between him and this Salih al-Fayyash in order to prevent him from hearing.

She continued on her way but soon paused before a vendor of powders and perfumes. She bargained a long

1. A *jebba* is a type of cloak.

time for something she eventually left without buying. Next she entered a cloth and clothing store, where the shopkeeper, who welcomed her with a greeting and a smile, began to show her textiles of different colors and patterns. He would open a bolt, spread it out, and display it in the sunlight and then in the shade while she examined each in turn, flipping them to see the reverse side. Then she left this shop to continue her peregrinations through the market, the boy beside her. To pass the time he watched the crowd around him: a man pushing a cart and another carrying on his head a basket filled with things, a beggar asking for alms, a blind man tapping the ground with his stick, vendors calling out their wares. Some offered straw hats or fans; others praised their perfumed extracts of orange blossoms, roses, and geraniums. There were roving auctioneers asking for the highest bid on an item, water-carriers, a man with a brazier of incense who was ready to fill a shop with fragrance, and a singer—accompanied by a drummer—who improvised songs of praise for those who paid and insulting satirical songs about those who refused—always to the same tune and starting with the same phrase. A brass ensemble passed, heading in the direction of Sidi Mahrez, and a newly circumcised boy in his magnificent gown followed them. A group of children crowded around him reciting: "Bear witness to God and glorify Him. / Muhammad, with prayer, sanctify him."

Shortly thereafter, she took the boy down another street where the commotion lulled and the hubbub subsided. The world of colors and motion slipped away like water draining through parted fingers. She branched off into smaller neighborhoods, proceeding along narrow, twisting alleys and other gloomy areas while he followed her silently and anxiously. Melancholy surged deep inside him. He wished that he could stay longer in those worlds swelling with clamor and agitation and that all the earth could be a sequence of uninterrupted souks.

When, after a long, exhausting trip through lonely streets, he noticed that she was finally leaving these for the Dar al-Basha district, his heart plummeted. He recognized this area at first glance. The girls' secondary school loomed before him. There were its large iron gate and the fenced garden from which tree limbs arched over the street.

This sight brought him out of his stupor. He looked around and shook his hand, trying to free it from the old woman's grip, perhaps intending to flee. Sensing this, she squeezed him rather roughly and threw him a stern look. "Where do you think you're going? Didn't you hear your mother tell you—even after we were in the street—not to let go of my hand a single moment?"

Her stern tone alarmed him. He could make out her features through her veil, and they seemed coarse, despite her fleshy cheeks, which normally gave her a lenient, affectionate appearance. He wiggled his hand again in her large fist, and his fingers fluttered like the wings of a sparrow wanting to fly off. But where would he go? She grasped him tightly.

He heard her say, "You seem to know the place."

Although he had a lump in his throat so big that he could not swallow, he replied, "Where are you taking me?"

"To your father." She said this with such determination that his face lost its color and became so pale that there seemed not a drop of blood left. His will to live deserted him, and he stammered in surprise, "No, I don't want to go there. I want to return to my mother. Take me back to Mother."

He burst into tears, and his wails resounded through the Dar al-Basha district. He stopped walking, began to fidget, and attempted to jerk his hand free of the woman's grasp. But in vain, for she held his fist in an iron grip. She shouted at him, "Good heavens! Don't embarrass me in public. Come on! Move it! Walk! Otherwise, I'll tell your father what you've done."

She yanked his hand so forcefully that she almost dislocated his shoulder.

3

$\mathcal{I}$t was almost noon, and sunshine glittered off the white walls, the light radiating into the deepest recesses. The heat of the day and the pace of life were both at a crescendo as people's commotion seemed most pronounced—whether the women in wraps, men in turbans and fezzes taking slow or quick steps, or the vendors making their rounds. Although Aunt Munjiya was bathed in sweat and panting from the heat, she kept doggedly to her route, not for a moment neglecting to keep an eye on the boy. Since her palm was slick with perspiration, his hand threatened to escape from hers, and she had to struggle repeatedly to recover it as she hurried on her way. Although obviously inconvenienced by the black veil covering her face and slowed by the white stole that enveloped her from head to toe, she was determined to deliver this boy, who had not stopped crying, to his father in the shortest possible time and thus to complete her mission. She had been the sole link remaining between the two families after his parents' divorce. Moreover, her calling as matchmaker and wedding hairdresser not only provided her access to every home and knowledge of every family but also made her an appropriate choice for missions of this delicate nature. All the same, this child, who would not stop crying, was starting to get on her nerves, not to mention the heat. Her patience exhausted, she yelled at him, "If you don't stop crying, I'll tell them everything you've done to me. So, hush!"

Gauging the sternness of her tone, he felt alarmed, fearing that she would complain to them. He recoiled nervously into himself and held back his tears until he choked on them and their salty taste filled his mouth. He stopped crying, and his soul shut itself off completely from the magical world of colors. He began to look at the world with gloomy eyes, for his previous experience with his father's family was imprinted on his mind as an indelible memory that would haunt him for years to come.

One afternoon, when the setting sun was throwing the courtyard into shadow, he and the other children were playing and shouting. There was not a care or worry troubling his mind. His mother was huddled with her sister, her grandmother, and her paternal uncle's wife and daughters around the tea tray, which held at its center the teakettle on a brazier. Their joyful laughter resounded to the heavens. This memory was still clear and pure, like a pristine mountain lake that no man's hand had ever touched. Then, all of a sudden, there was a knock on the door. The person who ran to open the door rushed back to Murtada's mother to announce a visitor. This was the first pebble thrown at that still surface, where it stirred up an agitated ripple. The women exchanged glances and then rushed off in every direction.

The human circle, which moments before had been unbroken, was scattered. A woman with wide eyes peered in from the hall door. They cautiously came forward to greet her. With a silk stole over her shoulder, she walked so majestically that her feet scarcely touched the earth. When his mother saw the woman, her steps faltered. Her voice became faint and distant as they exchanged greetings. While the other woman was temporarily distracted, his mother took him aside to whisper, "This is your grandmother. She has come to take you to your father."

The child had not been prepared for a surprise like this and had not been briefed on these complicated affairs. How could he go off with this grandmother about whom he knew nothing? Her wide eyes gazed at him severely, and she made no effort to smile or look cheerful. They escorted him to her and pushed him forward to kiss her. She presented her cheek to him coldly. He felt neither love nor hatred for her, neither affinity nor aversion. Her attributes and approach to life were totally unlike his mother's. Perhaps that was why his mother had not stayed with his father. Their marriage had lasted only two months before ending in divorce. This woman seemed a statue of wax or ivory or a wooden doll with wide blue eyes, a hollow voice that rose from deep within a well, and a mouth with an uneasy tilt to one side. She sat in an ostentatiously superior manner and was totally lacking in warmth.

This was a grandmother so unlike the typical grandmother that you would feel uncomfortable approaching her. Since he had known only his mother, what should he think? What was on her mind? What had brought her his way?

His mother took him aside to tell him about this woman, painting an attractive portrait and depicting her so positively that she convinced him. He fell for the trap and set off with his grandmother. After only a few steps, though, he turned on his heels, hardly suspecting that this wax statue possessed iron resolve.

She grabbed his hand forcefully and dashed off, dragging him across al-Hafir Street, while he filled the world with angry protests and wails. Then he began to bite and scratch her hands. She repaid him in full by hitting and pinching him. His mother watched this drama with tears in her eyes through a crack by the door. When she witnessed the abusive behavior to which this elegant woman resorted, she could not stand it and rushed to him, wresting him from that woman's claws and chastising her for this harsh treatment. She brought him back to the house, where he calmed down, recovered, and started to play again with the other children. That same evening, however, someone knocked on the door once more. This time it was a man with a furrowed brow and terrifying glances. When they told Murtada that this was his father, he left without protest. The man placed the boy in front of him on a humpbacked bicycle that traversed the streets without any procession or flourish and eventually conveyed him to a doorway somewhere. On alighting from the bicycle, he felt almost crippled by the pain caused by the bike's vibration during the trip. Thus his new life began with pain he endured without complaint.

He stealthily entered that house, which he had never seen before and where he knew no one. Although he ventured ever farther inside, no one greeted him. No one seemed to be at home. There were no voices or movements. Suddenly he came face-to-face with that wide-eyed woman, who was seated cross-legged on a dust-colored carpet all by herself in the loggia, at the center of the courtyard. He hesitated but eventually started toward her, because he saw no one else to approach. Her blue eyes shot him an angry glance that froze him in his tracks. He paused there anxiously, halfway to her, not knowing what to do or what was expected of him. Finding no one who would speak to him, he made his way to the wall, against which he could at least lean for shelter. From this vantage point he watched the movements of the man who had fetched him, the one they said was his father. He saw him enter a room silently and then emerge from it after removing some of his outer garments. Then the man headed to another corner of the house. When he came back toward the boy, he was carrying a stick. He grabbed the lad forcefully, laid him on his back, raised his feet to the sky, and rained painful blows upon the bare soles until he was breathless. He left the boy writhing in pain, hardly knowing what had happened. He pressed against the wall, hoping that its cool dampness would soothe his burning feet. As he glued himself to it, the boy felt the world grow blurred as he sank into himself. From that day forward, he felt that he had lost all sources of affection in the world. His heart was pervaded by a fear that would haunt him constantly for the rest of his life.

The harsh treatment he had experienced as a child of

no more than five, when he first met his father, made a deep impression and left him inclined toward melancholy. It cast an all-embracing but silent shadow over his soul. The bitterness of this experience stayed with him. He could not forget it even after they returned him to his mother for the duration of World War II, while it raged between the Axis forces and the Allies.

The war spread to encompass this sleepy land toward the end of 1942 and devastated it from one end to the other. The innocent inhabitants suffered, and the city of Tunis experienced various forms of bombardment, destruction, and death. Its residents fled for their lives from this calamity, group by group, seeking refuge with God's pious saints, heading for Sidi Ali al-Hattab, for al-Sayyida al-Manubiya, and also toward Hammam al-Anf to shelter with Sidi Buriqa, close to Sidi Moncef Bey, who took up residence in this region after the Axis forces reached an agreement with him to respect the neutrality of the town of Hammam al-Anf and the surrounding countryside. Wherever you sought refuge you would hear people reciting: "Gracious Qur'an-Revealer, be gracious to us. / We ask you for the Qur'an's sake and that of him to whom it was revealed."

All the same, the war, ever restless, spared no one and flooded these secure areas as well. Death and destruction pervaded them, reaching into the Bey's palace, for not even its status protected it from damage and aggression. He himself was subjected to curses and insults. Has anyone investigated these tragedies? Has anyone ever counted the innocent victims?

The events of those days left fault lines in people's beliefs and shook many of the notions they treasured. After violating the neutrality agreement, as they prepared to withdraw from Tunisia through the coastal region of Cap Bon at the beginning of May 1943, the Axis forces used the town of Hammam al-Anf as a base for fighting the advancing Allies.

This war left burning images that flashed through the boy's memory. One was of the time the air-raid sirens blew so wildly and repeatedly that panic and agitation filled the house. People raced around aimlessly, here and there. His uncle, sheltering himself against the wall of the courtyard, raised a hand toward the sky, pointing out something there. The boy clearly saw a jet-black airplane trailed by another that was a gleaming gray. This sight vanished quickly and was followed by the sound of a powerful explosion that rocked the whole city.

Another was when his mother, one night, took him from his bed and carried him out of their house to a reinforced concrete shelter they called "al-Sabat." They hid in there, in the dark, with a mixed group of men and women. He remembers that a neighbor, a man named Salah, took him from his mother and held him on his shoulder that night until the raid was over. Sometime after that, a report shook the whole neighborhood, spreading deep sorrow. He saw his mother weep. Salah had died in a bomber raid on the airport at al-Awena.

Many other random, splintered images were painted in his memory. One was of the night the English entered Tunis. He and his mother, fleeing from the war, had ended up with relatives, in Bab Sidi Abd al-Salam. That night some English soldiers broke the door when they attempted to tear it off its hinges. Drunk, they were on a rampage. Speaking a strange tongue, they yelled in harsh, hungry voices, looking for women. The people in the house were desperate. A gloomy silence held them in its sway, and their hearts were almost too frightened and terrified to beat.

Then the war stopped, or rather its chapter in Tunis ended. It was time for him to return from this exhilarating flight from the war with his mother. In the course of this journey, he had moved from the district of al-Halfaouine to al-Sayyida al-Manubiya and then from Bab Sidi Abd al-Salam to the suburb of Hammam al-Anf, a city that rises from the piedmont like a white lily, between the sea and Mount Bu Qarnayn. Its location places you at the winds' crossing and on the road that connects Tunisia's north to its south. The city astonishes you with the geometry of its streets and with its attractive central square. All roads branch out from there and return there. Palm trees line both sides of the principal street, which connects the mineral baths, the train station, and the Bey's palace to the extraordinary beach. His mother allowed him to run barefoot there, on the side streets or along the beach, all day long. There his eyes opened to the sea for the first time. He saw it stretch out, broad and blue, to the edge of the horizon. He was awestruck. The waves pounded the shore, one after another, while children played, sinking their bare feet into the sand and grubbing for shellfish. There were many interesting spots, sights beyond reckoning, and images that could never be erased.

How could his mother have betrayed him and surrendered him? She had told him, "You'll go on ahead of me to the bridal house with your Aunt Munjiya, because I have something to do. I'll meet you there in a while." For some time the family had been launching conversations about the wedding house when he was around, to lay the groundwork for what was to occur. They wove together strands of a story and sketched everything in perfect detail. Now he understood what was behind all those gestures, mysterious whispers, meaningful looks, and the other things that had awakened his fear and skepticism. Only now did he grasp the secret of the mournful tone in his mother's voice as she said good-bye to him, when she stood at the door and entrusted him to Aunt Munjiya.

Unable to rebel against him, she had obviously bowed to pressure from her uncle. He had frequently belabored this theme: "How long will this child remain with you? Do you want to raise him like a widow's child? Send the boy to his father. Find yourself another husband who can look after you. Do you plan to keep on this way? This isn't a life. I can't shoulder all these expenses any longer."

Her uncle would say this only to yield to compassion and relent when the decisive moment arrived. He had told her this before. The day she arrived on his doorstep pregnant he had refused to receive her in his house, and she had had to stay for a time with a maternal uncle with whom she had never been close, one who had never shown any affection or concern for her. He had a wife who was by nature tyrannical and who discovered in this niece a choice opportunity for displaying her nature. This aunt by marriage exploited the younger woman shamelessly, transforming her into little more than a servant. She made her do the housework, wash the dishes, and scrub the laundry. She consigned the pregnant woman to a room on the roof, which she reached laboriously by a narrow ladder, thrusting her belly before her. She lived in this way until it was almost time for the delivery. Then her grandmother interceded for her with her paternal uncle, who granted her permission to live with him, although he stipulated at the time that she should send the baby to its father the moment it was born. She had been forced to yield to this decree, bitter though it was.

The day Yamina went into labor, she pressed her fingers over her ears and told everyone around her, including her sister Dalila, "Take the newborn baby away from me, Dalila. Keep him away from me. I don't want to hear him cry, for that would bind him to my heart, only to have them tear him away from me. Take him far away. I don't want to hear his cries."

When her uncle heard this, his heart softened once more, and he came to the room's threshold. Standing there, drained of color, shaking like a reed from emotion, he told her, "Embrace your baby, Yamina. The piece of bread we divide four ways can be divided some more."

Yamina was stunned by this surprise. She clasped the child to her breast incredulously, sky-high with delight. When they searched for something to wrap around the newborn, they could find nothing. Then her sister Dalila thought of the cover on one of the beds. Seizing it immediately, she tore it into strips, and they wrapped him in some of that. Hope pulsed through his mother's heart once more and a smile brightened her face, to the delight of everyone in the household.

Thus another surprise had occurred, and the uncle's

soft side had emerged. Actually, he always gave in. If he appeared heartless, it was not by choice. By nature he was a good-hearted man, but he had difficulty coping with the pressures of daily life and the hardship of supporting a large family—ever in need of someone to provide them with food and other necessities—since no one else assisted him in bearing this burden or lent him a helping hand. Occasionally he treated his brother's two orphaned daughters a bit roughly when push came to shove. All the same, he was quick to yield when he could. A weaver, he had only what he produced with his two hands to buy bread. He had set up his loom in one room of the house, but his work did not exactly shower wealth upon him. His back was bent over his work all day long as he pounded against the batten on the loom. Then he would carry his weavings to sell in the market. Notwithstanding their poverty and the difficulties they had making ends meet, life in that house was free of fear. It was simple, joyful, and relaxed.

Aunt Munjiya maintained a firm grip on the boy's hand and a quick pace. The boy trailed behind her submissively, offering no resistance. There was no point in resisting when his mother wanted it that way and had, of her own free will, dispatched him to his father after deciding at last to free herself from him. Perhaps her last line of defense against her uncle had crumbled, but why had she resorted to this form of trickery and not discussed the matter with him or attempted to convince him that this was appropriate? Why had she deceived him? To whom could he fly? Where could he seek refuge?

As the house he had hated since he first went there

drew closer, step by step, his heart pounded faster and faster. When, finally, the woman stopped before the house, he felt his heart was stopping too. As she raised her hand to knock on the door, he began to tremble with fear. Searching for a safe place to hide, he snuggled up against the old woman's knees, since there was nowhere else. This time she embraced him, and her touch was light as she stroked his head, attempting to calm him. She asked about the piece of candy Salih al-Fayyash had bought him at Sidi Mahrez. He had let it drop from his hand on their way, for what good is candy when fear lends it a bitter taste?

4

Facing the bay, Dar al-Basha has squatted atop a hill, in the sea's embrace, from time immemorial, musing and looking down from its vantage point, where winds meet, routes converge, and cargoes arrive by land and by sea. There, between the snow-white domes of Sidi Mahrez and the minarets swimming through a deep blue sky, the call to prayer is raised. Over the towers of forts and at the gates of palaces, waves of light collide, dispersing colors, which are then diffused down alleyways and through the windows that overlook this landmark.

Murtada al-Shamikh continued through the district, pondering, rediscovering. The old sites returned to him after he had turned his back on them and struck off, in no particular direction, without goal or guide. He had experienced no peace of mind and no repose, for the world was tired of him, and he was tired of himself too. What an oppressive price he had paid! Many years had passed without any news of home, for he had seen no one to ask.

He had fled Dar al-Basha, heading he knew not where, and the fates had tossed him about before dashing him down on the high desert plains of a remote region of West Africa. In the vast reaches of Mauritania he had alighted and begun traversing the deserts—between Atar and Chinguetti—where tower bare, black boulders with tapered peaks scorched by the sun's flaming rays. Scattered rocks lie where they have fallen, cracked off from the boulders, nervous waves of sand undulate, storms erupt, and dusty winds rage, buffeting the boulders' tops. Distances are deceptive there, for the horizon pulses forward under a glowering sky. He had retreated to this wasteland as remote as that to which Prometheus was brought, shackled with heavy chains, to be fastened to the summit of a lofty crag. It was a place as remote as al-Mutannabi's refuge: "Leave me in a desert with no guide, / My face unveiled against the midday heat."[1]

There people whose faces overflowed with kindness eased his burdens. They opened their hearts and homes to him, insisting that he sit with them to dine or drink tea. These sturdy men wrap their faces against the sun's heat, and their narrow, black eyes sparkle like glowing coals. They live where the desert remains pure and unpolluted by petrol fumes.

From Chinguetti he went to Boutilimit, a land of giant sand dunes and of tents with flaps that sail open with the wind's gusts. Gazelles scatter in the distance, and at dusk

---

1. See al-Mutanabbi, *Diwan Shaykh Shua'ara' al-'Arabiya*, 371–75. Al-Mutanabbi (ca. 915–965), a renowned Arab poet, traveled from court to court as a panegyrist but spent time in the desert with Bedouins. He was eventually killed by some of them, apparently in revenge for a satirical poem directed at a clan member.

the herds of livestock return. Enormous, croaking ravens soar in the air. By night you hear the music of wedding celebrations. A shaykh moves from tent to tent, like a ghost, clutching his long, loose robe, repeating endlessly: "There is no god but God. . . . La ilaha illallah. . . . There is no god but God."

He thought the land so remote that no wayfarer would ever reach it. It was the kind of place he had always dreamed of visiting. He would live there, enjoying his isolation from human commotion. He might succeed in cleansing himself of all the filth adhering to him and, in the desert's embrace, discover time to experience peace of mind and to savor his fugue, the quiet, his dreams, and forgetfulness . . . in this infinite expanse where silence is replete with riddles and with the splendor of existence. Nothing matches the desert's labyrinth: that huge treasure trove of secrets, of the moon, of lying awake by night under a tent's flap till dawn breaks.

Then news he had not expected and would never have imagined took him by surprise: Salih al-Fayyash had suddenly appeared, as if the desert had spit him forth from its depths. When the children first brought the news, he had been reluctant to believe them. He had laughed sarcastically, for it seemed a fantasy or fairy tale concocted by them.

Who could confront these desert wastes and penetrate the infernal desert, save one previously scorched by the fires of Dar al-Basha? Even when the truth revealed itself clearly to him and he was face to face with Salih al-Fayyash, he choked in astonishment and nearly lost his mind. Despite the warmth of their meeting and embrace, he remained incredulous, retreating into a dream that seemed real, since reality played the dream.

Murtada al-Shamikh had endeavored to find a place so extraordinarily remote that no news of Dar al-Basha would ever reach him. Now Dar al-Basha had reached out across the desert to him, walking to him on its own two feet, in the person of Salih al-Fayyash.

He did not wait for the man to recover from his exhausting trip or to settle into a comfortable position. Murtada immediately asked, "How were you able to make it here?"

"I have come to exchange places with you."

"That's a cunning conundrum if I ever heard one."

"I make a serious proposal to you, and you label it a conundrum. Why?"

"You can exchange anything with me except place. This is the strangest thing I've ever heard."

"You seem to live totally cut off from news in this desert."

"Explain yourself more clearly. I don't understand you."

"The matter could not be clearer. I have come to exchange homelands with you."

"That's absurd too!"

"I tell you what's afoot and you term my statement absurd."

"But you and I are natives of the same homeland."

"I discuss the present, and you begin chatting about our past."

"How can two men exchange homelands?"

"There are diverse stratagems and multifarious ways.

Some exchange bodies, some wealth, some traditions and customs, some a language, but the annihilated dervish exchanges his spirit, and that is the weakest belief."

"Drop this obscurantism and tell me what you have in mind."

"What I have in mind is to take your place here in the desert while you return to Dar al-Basha to replace me there."

At this point Murtada shouted: "What's brought you here? Who showed you the way?"

"I have come to pay my respects to Shaykh Sidi Ya."

"Why do you need him?"

" 'Ask me no questions until I mention it to you.' "[2]

"Skip the phrases from the Qur'an and tell me why you've come."

"Only my Lord knows that."

"We return to your puzzles and cryptic phrasing."

"Sorry. If you prefer, I'll say nothing more."

He was quiet for a time. Then he rose, shook the dust from his long *jebba*, which was striped red and black, and pulled off the scarf that protected his face from the desert's midday heat. He removed his headgear, revealing a broad forehead and allowing his hair, which was flecked with white,[3] to flow down to his shoulders. He paused there,

---

2. Qur'an 18:70 (al-Kahf, meaning "the Cave"). In this Qur'anic narrative, a spiritual guide (popularly assumed to be Khidr) cautions Moses against leaping to conclusions.

3. See Qur'an 19:4 (Maryam, meaning "Mary"). This reference is to a self-deprecatory expression used in a prayer by Zakariya, father of John the Baptist.

gazing at the far horizon from beneath bushy, black eyebrows. His beard was white, and his face was wrinkled and puckered. He looked old and feeble.

He stood there at the center of the tent, motionless, for what seemed an eternity. The all-encompassing silence differed in no way from that of years past. Then he took his pack, threw it over his shoulder, and walked away without any comment or word of farewell. Alone, he headed into the unexplored reaches of the desert, disappearing as quickly as a passing breeze.

The Quarter

◆　　◆　　◆

"When They Ask You about the Mountains"

5

As he traversed Dar al-Basha's narrow streets, Murtada al-Shamikh felt he was being pulled endlessly down alleys that contract, broaden, twist, and intersect, beneath arches that multiply to infinity, past columns that succeed each other like alternating days and nights, and through sunshine that appears only to disappear. Looking down on him at every step of the way were walls decorated with colorful, ornamental patterns. Some of the painted stucco was peeling, while other surfaces held firm. He reveled in the ornamentation's antique beauty and faded grandeur.

Continuing on his way, he gently penetrated ever farther inside his old neighborhood. At a twist in the street he came upon a Qur'an school. The Dar al-Basha quarter is rife with Qur'an schools for primary pupils. This one's small door hung open, and its white steps led up to a jagged entrance like a cave's. The interior, far from being a cave's, brimmed with joy and light. He listened as children loudly chanted verses from the Qur'an to one another. He heard the voice of a student who was copying verses onto his slate: "Yes, master . . . 'When they ask you about the mountains. . . . ' "[1]

In a hoarse, off-key voice, the teacher prompted him: " 'Then say: My Lord will uproot them and scatter them like chaff. He will leave them level plains.' "

The boy repeated: " 'Then say: My Lord will uproot them and scatter them like chaff. He will leave them level plains.' "[2] The dictation continued as Murtada walked on.

High walls from other buildings threw a band of shadows across the opposite walls. Obscuring the light of the setting sun, they sketched evolving shapes and meandering lines, as the configurations of each roof's rim, with its alternations of acute angles and obtuse ones, left patches of light here and darkness there.

These wandering lines and angles, along with the sound of the teacher's dictation, stirred childhood memories of his Qur'an school: of being struck fiercely by the teacher's staff, of the slate covered from edge to edge with Qur'anic verses that he was expected to memorize and recite back to the teacher each evening before he was allowed to erase them and cover the slate with a watery slip of clay. The next morning his master would begin dictat-

---

1. Qur'an, 20:105 (Ta Ha).

2. Ibid., verses 105–6. In these two verses, Muhammad was instructed to respond to questions about the eternity of the physical world (represented by the mountains) in this manner: " 'My Lord will uproot them and scatter them as dust; He will leave them smooth and level plains.' "

ing all over again, and he would write out more appropriate verses of the Qur'an. Once his slate was full, he would
return to his place in the back with the other boys, at a
safe distance from the teacher's stick, to make it harder for
the man to hit him. Then he would start memorizing the
contents of his slate, reciting as loudly as the other pupils.

At first, the slate seemed tricky and uncooperative and
the verses inscribed on it incomprehensible, for they all
blurred together. Even so, he was expected to memorize
these verses well enough to recite them flawlessly, without
attempting to unravel their symbolism or to grasp the
meaning of any of the deeper passages. Indeed, the goal
was for him to memorize without understanding.

This treacherous operation cost him so much suffering, effort, and concentration that his young soul was oppressed and his spirit perplexed. He felt reduced to idiocy.
As a result, he grew up reading without comprehending
the meaning of words and listening to discourse without
understanding most of it.

The process was repeated each day for a period of
weeks, months, and years. The only relief from these tensions came when he observed through the school's window the shadows that appeared as the sun set, leaving
delicate traces on the walls of the surrounding buildings.
By this shadow he could predict their impending release
from the school's commotion and oppression, from the
excruciating pain of the stick's blows, and from the te-
dious effort of memorizing the slate's contents.

From school, his mind turned to the other recitation
sessions held at the ez-Zitouna Mosque. These were called

its "groups." Some recited the Qur'an after the morning prayer, some following the late afternoon prayer, and others between sunset and evening prayers.

He was expected to attend all these groups, since his father wished it and since it was thus a way to gain paternal approval. Any truancy would draw down his father's curse upon him, stoke the man's anger, elicit tough talk and rough treatment, and lead to deprivation of even the simplest things, like food, so that his life became miserable and his days as gloomy as his nights.

If for some reason he had to miss a morning session, it was imperative to attend in the evening, especially the group between sunset and evening prayers. He had begun to accompany his father to their assemblies as a novice, before he had learned the Qur'an, and continued to attend diligently for many years in unbroken succession, even after he had memorized the Qur'an, mastering it from start to finish. This circle, which was called the Downtrodden Group, favored a different style of Qur'an recitation. When they chanted, you would think them a group of men groaning as they combed wool or a corvée doing forced labor and dragging a heavy load with ropes while repeating monotonous, mournful chants—in call-and-response style—to help them raise that weight.

The boy was expected to hoist that weight every night. He was Sisyphus pushing a huge boulder repeatedly toward the summit of a mountain only to have it roll back to the bottom again, even though he had not committed any of the many offenses for which Sisyphus was punished.

Salih al-Fayyash was one of the regulars at these sessions. The warm friendship that linked him to the boy's father extended far back into the past and had grown stronger over the years. It was further reinforced by their shared interest in the spirit world, astrology, sorcery, and the magical arts.

The two men would leave the mosque together after the evening prayer and walk through the deserted souks, past stores that had closed for the night. They traversed the cloth merchants' market, the perfume vendors' market, and the souk reserved for leather slippers. Then they would enter al-Sayyida Ajula Street, all the while carrying on an uninterrupted conversation, resting occasionally, for a long or short time, before walking on. The two boys, Murtada and Munir, would trail after them, following in their footsteps, speeding up when the men did and stopping whenever they did. Once the two men reached Ramadan Bey Square, they would take leave of each other.

"Sleep well."

"Good night."

Murtada sensed something out of the ordinary in the way Salih al-Fayyash looked at him whenever he met the man or stepped forward to greet him. He noticed that Salih al-Fayyash showed a growing interest in him. He would look into the boy's eyes, as if attempting to penetrate deep inside to search for something there. The boy was so uncomfortable with this attention that he would hide his face and flee from these looks—like tongues of flame—although he never grasped their secret intent.

One day, after peering into the boy's eyes, Salih

al-Fayyash turned to Mr. Abd al-Jabbar and began to whisper to him, all the while glancing at the boy, who was certain they were talking about him.

The next day, Salih al-Fayyash came to their house following the afternoon prayer, took Murtada into a nearly dark corner of a room, and sat the boy down in front of him. With a pen, he started writing on the child's forehead in black ink. Next he tucked a piece of paper, which was covered with symbols, lines of writing, and bizarre inscriptions, inside Murtada's red wool *sheshya* cap.[3] Then he took the palm of the boy's right hand to write other things there in a circular pattern. In the center, he placed a large, glistening dot of black ink. They fetched a censer from which heavy, pungent incense belched. Then he asked the boy to gaze at the glistening black smear of ink: "Now you will tell me everything you see and hear in this dot of ink."

The boy scrutinized the gleaming black ink spot, studying it for a long time, not wresting his eyes from it or glancing to right or left. His hand was stretched out in front of him, and his head bowed. The man sat facing him. He interrogated the child, probing for information and urging him to look harder. He circled round the boy and sat down again, staring at him, while the incense filled the air, making the room's atmosphere oppressive. The boy's head grew dizzy, his neck pulsed with intense pain, his arm was exhausted, and his whole body suffered from this severe stress. Yet he saw nothing and heard nothing. All the same, the man was obviously unwilling to release him or

3. A *sheshya* is a traditional Tunisian felt cap.

to allow him a moment's rest. Salih al-Fayyash mumbled strange words, made ridiculous gestures with his hands, and insisted that the boy keep staring at the inkblot.

The pain in the boy's neck was excruciating, and he could no longer hold his arm up. His eyes began to dance in response to the dancing reflection of light from the black ink spot. Fear kept him from saying, "I can't take the pain." He could not think of any way out of this torment, given the man's unremitting determination and the terrifying glances from his father, who was seated in a corner, glaring at him. To escape, he would have to make up something from his imagination, inspired by the prompts Salih al-Fayyash had been providing him, however ludicrous they seemed. As the pain in his neck increased, he told the man, even though it was totally false: "I heard a voice say: 'Leave me now to the work I have in hand.' "

Thanks to this stratagem, Murtada was able to escape from the torment. They released him, and he raced from the stifling room to thrust his head toward the sky and inhale the fresh air, trying to ignore the pain in his neck. He went to cleanse all traces of the ink from his hand with soap and water, which he felt would wash away his humiliation as well. He could not believe the lengths to which they were willing to go to torment him and vanquish his spirit. After that incident, he became even more withdrawn and introverted.

He began to think that the next time they summoned him for this type of work he would refuse and tell them that he had not seen or heard anything, that he had lied to them, that he had invented what he said entirely from his own imagination, that he did not believe in their superstitions or in the jinn whom they sought to summon, and that he mocked all these projects. If he had to, he would flee from this ill-omened house the next time.

One night, however, when Murtada was dreaming sweetly, his father came, roused him from bed, and ordered him to dress. The boy looked around and saw that everyone else was asleep and that it was still night. He was puzzled by this situation and did not understand what was afoot. Sleep toyed with his eyelids, but all the same he allowed himself to be led away by his father, who walked him a short way in the gloom of the night down the desolate street, until they stopped in front of the house of their neighbor Uncle al-Arabi.

Then, with suspicious stealth and in a manner ripe with mystery, his father snuck him into this house. He brought the boy into a room and cautiously and quietly closed the door behind them. There the boy found himself face-to-face with Salih al-Fayyash. Now more than ever, the man's glances seemed fiery, gleaming, and terrifying. He started administering the familiar rituals. Then he began to ask the boy where the treasure lay. This time, however, the boy was unable to tell him anything, for sleep won out. The atmosphere of magic and talismans helped him succumb, and he abandoned himself to sleep's embrace. In the intense struggle, the boy seemed to have prevailed for a time, since they allowed him to sleep. Eventually they woke him again and asked for his assistance. He found that they had dug a deep hole in the ground. Dirt was piled in mounds at the side of the room, pieces of furniture were stacked on top of each other, and things were strewn about in a disorderly fashion. The group was tired and exhausted. They had failed miserably in their attempt to find the treasure, and the boy was unable to help them at this last watch of the night. He finally heard Aunt Duja, Uncle al-Arabi's wife, chastise the men: "Stop torturing the boy. If you can't find the treasure, how can this poor lad?"

6

$\mathcal{A}$s you proceed up the narrow streets of Dar al-Basha, you come upon Hammam al-Na'ura, the baths with the waterwheel. Over the low wall you see the mule, which is harnessed to the arm of the wheel with its eyes covered, plod in its customary circle to raise water from the depths of the well via a series of buckets leading to a trough that conveys water to the cistern.

Hammam al-Na'ura, which is reserved for women, is entered through a door painted green and red, as if this were a shrine dedicated to one of God's pious saints. You can catch the scent of women's warm bodies from its dark, covered galleries. The fragrance, which is mixed with the aromas of camphor, ambergris, gallnuts, and henna, is distributed throughout the area by the rising steam, stirring your emotions and awakening your imagination. You can hear the clink of containers being deposited and the basins being shifted about. You may even detect women's dreamy whispers if you listen carefully by the curtains covering the doors.

Our neighbor Uncle al-Arabi's home, which was near

the baths, had a special aroma and flavor all its own, for behind its simple facade were concealed forms of happiness totally unlike the tensions Murtada experienced in his father's house.

Whenever Uncle al-Arabi appeared at the door, exuding vitality and vigor, his booming voice would fill the house. As he entered, he stirred up a whirlwind of merriment. His wife Duja would hasten toward him, while his children—Tawfiq, Kulthum, and Shama—would also race to greet him, surrounding him on every side. One of them would relieve him of his basket and another take his burnous. He radiated buoyant vitality, and Duja would quiver with delight at his arrival, casting her magical spell over him. Convulsed with joy, he would exclaim: "Brave Duja, you're the sea and I'm a wave."

He loved telling her this, and she loved hearing him say it. Occasionally she would hide from him. When she heard him call, she would not respond. Then he would search for her everywhere, room by room. When he eventually found her, he would race to seize her by the waist and clasp her to him, sweeping her repeatedly in circles around the room, while saying over and over again: "Brave Duja, you're the sea and I'm a wave."

She would beg him coquettishly, "Put me down, Mr. al-Arabi. I'm going to faint."

Then he would hug her and shout, "Good gracious, Duja! Don't ever faint."

Murtada frequently visited Uncle al-Arabi's home. He would go there to draw water from their well on hot summer days or during Ramadan just before time to break the daily fast, for the water from their well was sweet and cold.

Occasionally they would send him there on an errand when no one else was around, and he would linger, playing with Shama, their youngest daughter. They played blind man's buff, jumped rope, or sat together on a stoop in front of the door to the hallway, watching a woodlouse roll itself into a ball and then straighten out. Shama loved to play, and Murtada loved Uncle al-Arabi's house.

Whenever he visited them, he found them cheerful and happy. Life at their house was different. It flowed limpidly, like pure water. Their glances were calm and never betrayed dread or fear. Their eyes shone with their smiles, and their memories were untarnished.

Shama would tell him about many delightful events in their lives. She told him about her father and mother and about her siblings. She would giggle and break into gales of laughter. Murtada listened to her without laughing. He could think of nothing to tell her, since life in his household was different.

People did not smile there. When Murtada attempted to remember his home and his first days there, he confronted a frightening void. No matter how hard he tried to stir his imagination, he found nothing. He remembered none of the members of his household. He did not even remember anything about his father. He might just as well have never seen him, even though the man dominated the whole dwelling. Murtada lived there neglected and isolated, like a specter or a phantom, wandering through life at several paces' remove.

He had a gap in his memory, as if there had been a sudden failure, exactly like that of a defective tape recorder. You see the tape turn and the reel revolve, but when you wish to hear the sound, you discover that the machine has recorded nothing, because of damage to the instrument or a defect.

What did he do there? Where did the members of his family lurk? He did not remember anyone and could not dredge up anything, although he still remembered everything that had happened when he lived with his mother, down to the tiniest detail, even though he had been younger when he lived with her.

Some terrifying lapse had occurred in his memory so that no matter how hard he exercised his imagination, he met a gaping void and felt panic-stricken. This deep fissure kept him from experiencing pleasant dreams and denied him enjoyment of a happy childhood. By causing him to lose his taste for sleep, it nearly destroyed him. A sense of deprivation settled in his heart along with an inescapable feeling of alienation. He experienced a blurry amnesia.

What had happened? Conceivably, he had succumbed to an extremely premature form of senility caused by the stress of his first meeting with them. That rude shock had plunged him into a world of forgetfulness. Afterward, he had lived as if his spirit were errant, his soul oblivious, and his imagination diseased, but in the still of the night, after he had slipped into bed under his cover, he would try to remember. Bitter tears would stream silently from his eyes. Even so, one night, one of them had caught him at this, jerked the cover off, and rebuked him harshly and sarcastically. The tears in his eyes not only faded away, they dried up completely. From that time on he neither wept nor laughed.

His sweetest moments came when a storm disrupted the electricity and darkness prevailed. Then their staring eyes and their stern faces would vanish as they scurried off in search of candles. How beautiful candlelight was! The dancing wick allowed imaginary shapes to waltz across the walls. Only at those times did his memory return. He would feel then that he belonged to this household, as their voices touched him from afar. Perhaps harsh light—bouncing rudely off every surface—creates tension and coldness between people, strains nerves relentlessly, and turns you into an object to be inspected, a suspect to be cross-examined. When the light grows dim, eyes renounce their ceaseless, inquisitive stares and people's nerves can settle, allowing mutual understanding to reign.

Oh, what happiness overwhelmed him once! His grandmother unexpectedly showed him some kindness, noticed his existence, and gently rested her hand on his head, after he had never ventured near her and she had not so much as looked at him. That evening, once she had put his brother Munir to bed as usual, she called him. Placing his pillow on her feet, she began to rock him to sleep, alternating her legs to move his head to the right and then to the left. On another occasion, she brought warm water to wash his brother's feet and—when she saw him standing watching her—invited him to come so she could wash his feet, too. When she began to pass her hand over the sole of his foot, the tickling sent a tingle up his spine. He shivered and could scarcely restrain his laughter.

His brother Munir had lived there longer than he had, although Munir's mother was their father's second wife. Perhaps his mother was luckier. She had stayed with her husband for two years and had given birth to her child during that period. The gleam of his smile spread delight and contentment through the family, since he was the first child born in the house to the custody of both parents and into the safekeeping of his grandmother. Their happiness was even greater, since they had been deprived of the first child, who had been born far away.

The father, Abd al-Jabbar, however, soon divorced this second wife, who carried off her child, leaving the household devastated.[1] It was not clear whether Abd al-Jabbar subsequently regretted the divorce bitterly or came to hate this wife so much that he resolved to punish her in an exemplary way. In any event, he decided to steal the child from the mother without any warning to her. Accounts as to the circumstances vary and contradict each other.

The most commonly accepted version is that he found the child wandering alone in an alley in the middle of the old city and brought the poor little boy, who was no more than two, home with him, without telling the boy's mother. The child was in a sorry condition, so they said, ill and filthy, his belly distended, with such severe diarrhea that he had puddles around his feet. The grandmother took charge of the child, opening her arms to him, from the very first day. She lavished love and affection on him and supervised his rearing. He even slept in her room.

---

1. Qur'an 2:259 (al-Baqara, meaning "the Cow"). This verse is a parable about God's ability to resurrect and restore people and cities. The despairing phrase echoed in the chapter, therefore, comes with a silver lining.

Their grandmother's room—unlike the rest of the house—was decorated with precious items. There were rows of chests, a high bed, mirrors opposite each other, drapes, a box inlaid with mother-of-pearl, chairs with high backs, vessels, amulets, carpets, a brass lamp, a silver censer, carafes and glasses, a porcelain platter, pillows, and clothing. A many-armed chandelier hung from the ceiling. Prominently displayed on the wall were a large grandfather clock, ancient daggers, and a sword set with gemstones.

In the center of that wall was a life-size, full-length portrait of his grandfather. The man sported a handlebar mustache and a confident gaze. He stood erect in his military dress uniform with embroidered stripes on the shoulder. On his head was a tall cap, and a sword hung by his side. He gripped the handle of the sword as if he were a Turkish sultan.

Murtada liked to stand in front of this painting of his grandfather and stare at it. They had told him strange tales about his grandfather, but these were always abbreviated and filled with riddles and mysteries, which fascinated him all the more. He wanted further information, but this was futile, for he could never find anyone who would quench his thirst or slake it.

At disparate, disconnected times he heard them talk with great distress and pain about his grandfather. Then they would suddenly change the subject without clearing away any of the secrecy that continued to cloud his grandfather's life. Murtada's aimless mental peregrinations continued as he attempted to reconcile his grandfather's image that hung on the wall with his grandfather as he really was. He tried to solve this riddle and to discover what had actually happened.

Murtada would look at his grandmother and study her physique, which was fashioned from ivory, and her beauty, which had not faded even as she aged. He was perturbed by her large, mystifying, blue eyes, which she had hoarded for herself alone and had not passed on to any of her descendants. He would gaze at her and ask in secret agony, "What did you do to my grandfather that caused him to die in a distant land and contributed to whatever else happened to him? He died alone and deserted, and they buried him in a cemetery for foreigners. Then you monopolized your only son, who lived in such total dependence on you that he grew up in this nervous, wretched, peculiar fashion. Now I, your grandson, am afflicted by what afflicted my grandfather, seared by the same fire that seared him."

They said that before he married her, he had never tasted wine, had guarded himself against its temptations, and had shunned those who surrendered to it. So what had induced him to try wine, prompting him to drink it eagerly, as if attempting to make up for everything he had missed? He had become so addicted to alcohol that it devastated his life.

One day he took her to a charitable institution, where he left her, and volunteered for the army. Her father had been forced to take the matter before a judge. On the day of the hearing, Murtada's grandfather appeared wearing his uniform and observed craftily: "As you can see, your honor, I am now in the armed services."

The judge cast him a knowing glance and declared,

"Settlement of this case is postponed until he's discharged from the army."

Her father took her from the charity home, and she remained in suspended animation, neither married nor divorced, until the end of World War I.

Murtada's grandfather knocked on her door one day and told her, "Taja, if you wish to come back, your house is open, but I won't tolerate any discussion of the past. Don't ask me what's happened."

So the two were reunited, and they say he gave her a valuable necklace. It was not long, however, before he started drinking, even more heavily than before. They report that he could drink a great deal without losing his balance or his dignity.

One night he drank far more than usual, became intoxicated, and returned home gloomy and preoccupied. He retreated to a far corner of the house, without saying anything to Taja or even looking at her. The next morning he went out to obtain divorce papers. He sent her back to her father's house, just like that, for no apparent reason.

He left the children with her and disappeared suddenly from sight. No one ever saw him anywhere again. Later on, reports surfaced that he had gone north to Bizerte to reenlist.

It was not long before other news reached them: that he was in the military hospital and very ill. After that, the flow of information was interrupted once more, and what they did hear was contradictory. Some said that he had been seen at the harbor, preparing to board a steamship to travel overseas. Others said that he had died and that they had buried him in a foreign cemetery facing the bay of Bizerte.

Such was the life—filled with amazing fluctuations and strange incidents—that his grandfather had lived. It remained enveloped in obscurity and mystery, a sealed secret that could not be penetrated. Quite possibly its repercussions had influenced the general atmosphere pervading the life of this family. This was the secret that continued to torment Murtada, keeping him awake at night and driving him to search for clues far and wide.

Aunt Haluma, who apparently wanted to clear up the confusions about this case and to remove the suspicions from Murtada's head, since he kept coming to her with insistent inquiries, would say, "Listen, son: don't wear yourself out trying to find out what happened to your grandfather. They say this all occurred because of a glass of wine presented to him that night by a man called Mooh, who had once quarreled with your grandfather. Because of that dispute, your grandfather had stopped patronizing the bar Mooh frequented and had begun going to a nearby tavern. On that ill-omened night, while your grandfather and a group of his friends were celebrating the anniversary of his return from the war and everyone was elated and happy, the waiter from the other bar arrived to offer him a drink, saying, 'This drink's on Mooh, who offers you a toast in honor of your celebration.'

"In the flush of inebriation, in that party atmosphere, surrounded by clamorous drinkers, your grandfather accepted the glass, put it to his lips, and drained it in a single gulp, without considering what he was doing. Then he set down the glass and immediately began to slap his head, shocked that he had accepted, from his foe, a full glass brought in from the other bar.

"It was this incident that turned his life upside down, for what happened later was on account of that glass, which was presented to him by his foe and which he drained. That drink set his heart on fire, sent him wandering to distant ports, and turned him into a vagrant. In the end, he died and was buried without mourners or a proper funeral."

Murtada had no doubts about the strong friendship that bound his grandmother to Aunt Haluma, who visited his grandmother almost daily during some periods. At other times, if her visits had ceased for a lengthy stretch, his grandmother would send him out to check on her.

Her house was tucked into an odd corner. It was situated on Barans, a narrow lane leading into Sidi Mafraj Street, which connects to the Jewish neighborhood of al-Hafsiya and pours into Ramadan Bey Square. After that, there is a fork from which al-Basha Street branches off.

Aunt Haluma would call on his grandmother almost every day, following the afternoon prayer. She would rap on the door in her special way. Although exhausted, she would wait at the door and only enter if she found her friend in. Otherwise, she would return home.

His grandmother would hurry to welcome her and insist that she enter. She would come inside, staggering with fatigue, and attempt to pull herself together. His grandmother would take her to the sitting room, where she would collapse onto the nearest seat. She would pant there for a while until she caught her breath. Then she would inquire of his grandmother, with anxious eyes and in a low voice, whether anyone else was at home before the two women began to share their secrets. If his grandmother heard the door open or approaching footsteps, she would stretch out her hand to touch the knee of Aunt Haluma, who would change the topic of conversation. They would continue chatting until after the evening prayer. When it was time for the guest to leave, his grandmother would see her to the door, where they enacted nearly the same scene each time: "God willing, we'll soon celebrate Ahmad's return."

"I'm so upset about Ahmad. I don't know where he is or what land has swallowed him."

"Those absent must return one day."

"I'm so upset. Ahmad's absence has lasted such a long time, Sister Taja."

Everyone in the neighborhood knew Ahmad's story. All the way from the district of al-Hafsiya to Dar al-Basha, one person would tell another the tale. Ahmad had been in the prime of his youth, bubbling with vitality and energy. He had been a source of delight and happiness for his parents, who were of modest means. He was the only child remaining to them after death had swept away all their other offspring. He was their only hope, the light of their eyes. They would gaze at him and pray that God would preserve him from all harm.

Ahmad would fill the air of al-Hafsiya with noise and commotion, pushing his cart before him and offering passersby vegetables and fruits of all shapes and colors. He would wash them, sort them, put them in piles, arrange them by color as if painting a picture, and place a bouquet of roses atop them. Then he would tuck behind one ear a nosegay of jasmine blossoms and call out in his mellow voice:

> I have apricots.
> I got sunstroke collecting them;
> Yet I'm giving them away:
> Even their pits are worth more than my price.

He advertised apples in this way:

> My son,
> Here's a fragrant fruit that
> Gives spirit to your soul.

He knew how to display his produce, just as he knew the right fruit for each season, the appropriate call for each fruit, and the right garb for each occasion.

He lived in this way, as the days passed, until he heard some despicable news: the report that on November 29, 1947, the United Nations had ordered the partition of Palestine. The report took on a life of its own and spread. So much attention was focused on it that eventually the people's anger exploded and men began to volunteer to fight in Palestine against the Zionist invasion forces. Ahmad was in the first group of these volunteers. His mother begged him repeatedly to stay home, stroking his head and kissing his forehead, but he would laugh and kiss her. Looking at her, he would calm her by saying, "It's just for a short time while I will do my duty and then I'll return to you."

Her mind was at rest when she bade him farewell with trilling ululations. Then she hunkered down to await his return. Days passed, the summer went by, and seasons and years skipped away, while Aunt Haluma continued to wait. People would still attempt to comfort her by saying, "God willing, we'll soon celebrate Ahmad's return."

7

*N*ow you are returning to Dar al-Basha, disoriented and exhausted. Yes, you are weighed down by your experiences, but you have an increased capacity for endurance. You will endure whatever confronts you and any difficulties that bar your way.

You return a changed man, after wandering aimlessly for a long time. You erred down all kinds of roads until you bottomed out and renounced your self. Long years passed during which you did not savor any stability or know, even for a single day, the meaning of the word *repose*, because of the trials you confronted and the ruinous condition of your spirit.

· The fire of passion flamed inside you as you searched for some reprieve from the accursed spirit pervading you. It was borne by a detestable cell that gnawed at your bones without giving the least hint of a truce. You were absent for a long time, living in a daze, tossed about by anxiety, your head haunted by apprehensions.

You set forth fragmented, exiled for your ideas, pursuing fantasies and phantasms. You were shunted hither and thither, between different climes and capitals, as different languages jumbled together on your tongue, both Eastern and Western ones: from Paris to London, from Geneva to Bonn, from Rome to Belgrade, from Athens to Sofia to Istanbul, and then on to Baghdad. From there to Tehran, then Damascus and Beirut. Then Cairo. After that to Andalusia and Madrid. Then to Moscow and Leningrad, then Minsk, and from there to Tashkent, followed by Samarkand and Bukhara, then Nouakchott and Dakar. You were tossed about like a straw and trembled so convulsively that you fell into a trance. Unable to tell one path from another, you lost your self-control and your balance. Your existence was shaken to its roots, until you denied all your beliefs and suffered severe culture shock. You were reduced to a stupor and thus seemed stupid, until eventually you cast what was left of you into the infernal desert.

You discovered that you were no more capable of returning to Dar al-Basha with your heart at peace than of washing your hands of it or of taking a break from thinking about it. What should you do? How should you relieve yourself of your anxiety and torment? You needed either to return to Dar al-Basha with a new heart or to free yourself of it without freeing yourself from your anxiety.

Abu Bakr al-Shibli described your condition when he said:

I'm so troubled by you, I'm not even conscious of my trouble,
You're the cure of my illness, even though you're its cause. . . .
I've repented countless times, but since meeting you,
    repentance is pointless.

It hurts as much to be near you as far away; so when will I find
   any peace?[1]

You went out in search of deliverance, not caring what
difficulties might confront you on your way. You were
buoyed by elation, the elation of deliverance from Dar
al-Basha, from the pressure of its fetters, from its customs
and an incessant subjugation that humiliated you until
you could bear it no longer.

You were not adequately armed, since Dar al-Basha's
domination had prevented you from providing yourself
with any weapons. You set forth, not knowing what path
you ought to follow. Since you were callow and inexperi-
enced, you stumbled right away. Your every project failed
miserably, perhaps because you fought with a blunted
weapon and a broken soul. All the same, you did not sur-
render, and that is the important thing. You kept on fighting and steeling yourself for disasters, until they no longer
frightened you.

You were keen to triumph first over your self—since it
was the sole impediment to your progress—and to strip it
of timidity and fear. You also had to cut through the veil of
custom and pioneer a new path far removed from any
oversight. You had to attempt all this, even if it led to dis-
mal failure.

---

1. Abu Bakr al-Shibli, *Diwan Abi Bakr al-Shibli* (Abu Bakr al-Shibli's Collected Poems), 36. This love poem is open to religious inter-
pretation with God playing the role of the poet's Beloved; Murtada's
Beloved is the Dar al-Basha neighborhood. Al-Shibli (861–945) was a
Sufi master, a friend of al-Junayd and al-Hallaj, and the onetime gover-
nor of Nahavand. He ended his life in an asylum, still teaching Sufism.

You had to cleanse your mind of any memories of your subjugated childhood, which began with the first pain you bore patiently when you were denied a chance to scream or moan, let alone protest. You were forced to bear your pain in silence. All sorts of pain can be borne patiently, but what is intolerable is being forced to bear it silently. That is the harshest form of subjugation for the soul. You had to forget that accursed past and to distance yourself from it in order to liberate yourself. In exactly the same way, you had to tread on live coals and endure your separation from your mother when they wrested you away from her by force and refused to provide you with any news of her. They would not so much as mention her name in your presence, as if it were a dirty word. They would say "Your Aunt So-and-So." When they made some belittling remark about her behind your back, your ears honed in on that insult while your eyes did not know where to look. You detected the faintest whisper or gesture that referred to your mother. What can a child of five do when he suddenly finds himself in a household where he knows no one? To prevent her memory from becoming a lump in your throat or keeping you awake all night long, you made a deliberate effort to conceal that secret in your bosom, not mentioning it to anyone. That is what you did as well, afterward, with the Qur'an verses you memorized in Qur'an school, with what you learned from works of jurisprudence, metaphysics, theology, and Arabic grammar, and from long-winded commentaries in all those other yellowed books. That is what you did with what you garnered from texts, commentaries, and marginal notes, especially from grammar treatises and syntactical discussions, like the beginning of Ibn Malik's *Alfiya*: "Our speech is an instructive phoneme like 'Rise!' and a noun, a verb and then a particle."[2]

In Ibn Hisham's commentary, which is called *Dripping Dew and Quenching Thirst,* you find: "The author says: 'a word is an indivisible statement.' The commentator says: 'Word is used to refer to a self-sufficient phrase as when God Almighty stated: 'By no means! It is but a word he says.'[3] The reference here is to God's statement: 'O my Lord! Send me back [to life] so I may rectify the things I neglected.' "[4]

You wend your way through subordinate clauses that resemble Dar al-Basha's twisting and turning maze of interconnected streets and dead-end alleys. You continue with the commentary: "What is meant by 'statement' is a phoneme that refers to a concept. . . . A 'phoneme' is a sound that includes more than one consonant or vowel and that may refer to a concept . . . or that, like *dyaz,* which is Zayd spelled backwards, may not. . . .[5] If you ask, 'Why did you specify that a word should have a conventional meaning . . . ' I reply: They required that because

2. Ibn Malik, *Alfiya Ibn Malik* (Ibn Malik's Poem in a Thousand Lines), 3. Ibn Malik (ca. 1203–1274), who came from al-Andalus but settled in Damascus, where he taught the Islamic sciences, is famous for his works on grammar.

3. Qur'an 23:100 (al-Mu'minun, meaning "the Believers")

4. Ibid., 23:99–100. As the text explains, the message here is that we should shun evil now, while alive, and not hope for a second chance to set things straight in this material world.

5. Abd Allah Ibn Yusuf Ibn Hisham, *Qatr al-Nada wa-Ball al-Sada,* 13. Ibn Hisham (1310–1360) was a grammarian who lived in Cairo.

they considered phoneme to be the genus for word."[6] Then you progress through the science of phonetics, studying which phonemes may be used and which may not and their division into the clearly enunciated versus the whispered and between phonemes of rising or descending intonation. You discover that they specified in the definition of "speech" that it must be instructive.[7] This discussion includes a response to anyone who would argue that "speech" is the act of the speaker or that it is a concept that inheres in the soul, as well as subsections devoted to "speaker" and the true meaning of this term, followed by the division of speech into obsolete and current, and so on to the end. This discussion only gained in complexity, convolutions, and gyrations the further it advanced and as differences multiplied between the citizens of Basra and the people of Kufa, between grammarians like Sibawayh, al-Kisa'i, al-Akhfash, al-Zamakhshari, al-Mazini, and al-Mubarrad.

Traditional Islamic linguistics resembles the dress of the traditional Islamic shaykh, who sports a turban, which is wrapped around the *sheshya* on his head, a heavy burnous, cut wide and worn over a flowing *jebba*, below which traditional trousers, or *sirwal*, hang down to his ankles in a thousand and one folds and pleats. Over his trousers, around his waist, is wrapped a long sash, like a rope for the bucket of a well. Above the sash is the sleeveless vest, under which are worn a long-sleeved vest and a shirt. On his feet are yellow leather shoes, black slippers,

6. Ibid., 14.
7. Ibid., 35.

and stockings. All of this is to say that there exists a syllogistic relationship, a concord, and a harmony between the city's souks (with their web of interconnecting alleys and walls), its dwellings, the attire of its scholars and of local notables, and their grammar, jurisprudence, theology, and literary works, which mix concision with pomp and haphazard accumulation with gravity.

There are many other examples among works you memorized, made part of your life, and learned, including all the books that the shaykhs of ez-Zitouna Mosque dictated to you. You were unable to find anything to help you confront this changing life or these difficult times in this education.

It is true that all this filled you with an awesome spiritual strength, which enabled you to hold your head up the whole time—despite the destructive blows raining down on you—and to stand on your own feet. All the same, it convulsed your being and destroyed your self-confidence. Thus you became withdrawn and licked the bitter taste of your defeats. With your frowning face and anxious glances, you began to feel alienated, and your life was as good as ruined.

Yes, to be sure, this education was able to transport you beyond the limiting frame of your own small country to distant horizons so that you lived with your eyes constantly focused on the great empire the length and breadth of which you were able to traverse, speaking a single language and moving freely from one set of boundaries to another, from the land of the Tigris and Euphrates rivers in the east to the shores of Mauritania in the west, with all sorts of environments in between and countless cities, from urban centers to nomadic peoples, from palace to tent, from popular republics to conservative caliphates, from minarets to cabarets, and from obscene splendor to crushing poverty.

The Half

+   +   +

Trackless Time

8

*P*rogressing through Dar al-Basha, Murtada shivered as shafts of light spilled over the roofs of the buildings and sunshine glistened off walls and crannies filled with marvels. His heart pounded, and he felt a powerful connection and craving for the district and its unusual scenes, which were so familiar to him, like that old woman, still carrying wool to sell in the Souk al-Tu'ma.

He had no idea where his footsteps would lead him. He was breathing heavily as he explored and investigated. He might just as well have been confronted by one of those puzzling scenes he had beheld on peering into a peepshow's world of marvels, pressing his eyes against the holes in the box. He had felt the same way when Uncle Mansur al-Shamikh had taken him to al-Halfaouine Square during one of the illuminated Ramadan nights, which were full of delight and enjoyment. Then he would enter the children's play area, climb on a swing, and soar high into the air. He would ride the horses on the merry-go-round and afterward thrill to the somersault ride that carried him to the dome of heaven. He could almost touch the candles on the brightly lit minaret of the Master of the Seal Mosque. Then he would purchase a ticket for the Karagoz shadow-puppet theater, where he would sit on one of the tall wooden chairs lined up in rows while—with a red tongue—he sucked a candy called "ghoul's treat" and watched Isma'il Pasha. He would watch the heroes debate, fight, and then draw their swords. He would scream with delight, clap, and laugh, because Isma'il Pasha was victorious over the scoundrels, defeating them all.

Uncle Mansur was a different type of man, totally unlike anyone else in that household. His room, which was next to the hallway, was always open to the sun. Its furnishings were simple: a bed, a wardrobe, and a chair.

He spent the greater part of his day away from the house. He would leave early in the morning and return only late at night. At times he would be absent for a few days or even weeks before returning. He would announce his arrival by clearing his throat from a distance to avoid taking members of the household by surprise or embarrassing them in any way. He would also clear his throat when he was about to enter the bathroom or perform some other act of personal hygiene. On the extremely rare occasions when he did stay home, he would spend the whole day squatting in his room without leaving it.

He did not mingle with his relatives in the house except on feast days and during the glorious month of Ramadan, when he would sit at table in the evening to break his fast with the others. They treated him inconsiderately and even harshly at times. He was conscious of that and endured it silently, without allowing the least word of protest to escape his lips or even moving an eyelid. He was treated this way even though his proprietary rights to the house were identical to those of Mr. Abd al-Jabbar. Ownership of the house was now shared equally by the children of the three brothers: Abd al-Jabbar al-Shamikh, Mansur al-Shamikh, and al-Hadi al-Shamikh, for each to husband as he saw fit.

Al-Hadi, however, had left the house years before, ever since he took a job as an employee in the Finance Ministry. He had left the first chance he got, moving with his wife and young children to a home in a new community in the suburb of Bardo, where he had a modern villa with a garden full of fruit trees and flowers. He was not condemned, as he was wont to say, to spend his whole life in a wretched house frequented by ghosts of the past.

Al-Hadi lived differently and looked different, too, for he was very dapper and always sported a new suit, a bow tie, and gleaming new shoes, so that he looked as if he had just returned from a magnificent reception where he had had a delightful time. He paid visits to the family at scattered intervals. Everyone would welcome him with great courtesy and go to extra pains to honor him. All the same, he would not stay seated long, moving about all the time, never resting in one spot.

His eyelashes were as black as the night, so that you could easily imagine he used kohl around his eyes. Wavy, with not a strand out of place, his hair glistened as if well greased. His part, which was carefully demarcated, ran true down the middle of his head.

His children—Abd al-Sattar, Nur al-Din, and Radiya—all studied at the Lycée Carnot. They always spoke French, everywhere, even when they were quarreling. When their maternal aunt visited them, they would call her "Tata," even though the poor woman was offended by this French slang. She would shout at them, "I don't want to hear this name that's only fit for dogs. Call me Khalati. Use Arabic!"

Uncle Mansur had always occupied this room, off the hallway, but his wife had died, leaving him with a daughter, named Zuhra. Zuhra had grown to be an adult without any man ever knocking on her door and thus had missed the wedding coach. Perhaps she was not pretty enough. She lived in a constant state of bewilderment but was always ready to undertake any task, hastening to do chores, even unbidden.

Throughout the day she moved as consistently as the pendulum of a clock, without showing any signs of fatigue or exhaustion. With her continuous, unceasing activity, she seemed to be trying to compensate for what had escaped her in life. She was unconcerned about her own affairs and paid no attention to her appearance. Her clothes were simple but always clean. Her forehead was wide and protruding, and her hair rose in dancing spirals. Thin and brown, she moved like a pale shadow or a specter. If you asked her about something she would respond, and if you sought anything she would swiftly bring it to you.

Zuhra had seizures during which she fainted, and these might occur at any hour of the day or night, for no apparent reason. Her body would quiver, her limbs stiffen, and her teeth knock together. White foam would spurt from the corners of her mouth, flow over her chin, and course down her cheeks. Her eyeballs would bulge out toward the ceiling, and she would release a loud scream before falling into a swoon. Her extremities would already have stiffened by the time they rushed to her. They would search for a large key, which they tucked into her fist and then rotated back and forth inside her grip until she relaxed and gradually returned to normal. All the same, for the rest of the day, she would have a yellow face, feel sick, and move with difficulty.

Zuhra slept in the sitting room, and Murtada slept there too. She was fond of him and understood whatever he felt without having to discuss it or say a word. She was by nature more partial to work than to words and used actions and deeds to express her opinions. When people addressed her, she would stammer and not know how to reply. Her rights were frequently abused and abridged, because she had difficulty defending herself.

Murtada would never forget her courageous support and her death-defying defense of him once when his father punished him for something he could no longer remember. When everything is said and done, it was some piddling infraction. Anyone living under those pressures and in comparable fear naturally develops into a powerless creature incapable of committing a foul deed that actually merits punishment, even if fear itself occasionally drives him to commit some blunder.

Murtada forgot what the trivial offense was, but he would never forget the cruel punishment his father inflicted on him. One night he shackled the boy with chains, took him to the roof, and threw him into a deserted storage room. He left the boy alone there, turned the light off, and came back downstairs.

Zuhra wasted no time in climbing right up there. She freed Murtada from the chains and brought him down from the roof terrace so brazenly that he shook with fear more for her sake than his own. She did that in front of all of them, to their utter astonishment, thereby challenging the will of Mr. Abd al-Jabbar, who made everyone else in the house cringe. No one ever dared to disobey his command or defy his will.

Zuhra was quivering like a windswept reed. Her hair looked like uncoiled springs, and her eyes wildly scanned the room without focusing on anything. Her nose was sniffing and her lower lip trembling. She was clutching Murtada and hugging him. She was on the alert and fully prepared to react to any provocation.

They had all stopped what they were doing to observe this spectacle silently. They saw Mr. Abd al-Jabbar advance, sparks flying from his eyes. Their hearts pounded with fear for the imminent disaster, but before he could reach her, something no one had anticipated occurred. Zuhra emitted a single shriek and fainted dead away. She had one of her typical seizures that could strike her at any moment, but this one was the worst she had ever experienced. She began to writhe, pounding her body against the floor. So much white foam poured from the sides of her mouth that they thought she was dying.

Confronted by this wild scene of agitation and by the alarm felt by all the family members, including Mr. Abd al-Jabbar (who began to recite passages from the Qur'an for her), Murtada feared he was responsible for everything that had happened. He stood at the bottom of the stairs that led to the roof, feeling miserable and gaping at the concentrated gloom, not knowing how to escape or where to seek refuge. He began to scream and scream and scream and scream, hoping he would suffer a seizure like Zuhra's. Perhaps that would rescue him from the multifarious punishments he anticipated. Aren't the best solutions at times the most outrageous ones?

Salih al-Fayyash arrived—for he was the spiritual physician who watched over the souls of the neighborhood—and proclaimed, "This is the work of the jinn. The only way she can free herself is to visit the shrine of Sidi Bin Isa in al-Qallalin Square near the Carthage Gate, every Friday following the afternoon prayer. She needs to repeat that for seven consecutive weeks."

Murtada was Zuhra's devoted and constant companion when she visited this shrine, where women entered special enclosures reserved for them and men sat in two long lines that faced each other and curved to form perfect circles, in the center of which sat their Sufi master.

The men began by performing various prayers and rituals to a steady beat with regular movements. That phase culminated with invocations to a series of saints and numerous hymns. Then they recited selections from the Qur'an and plunged into the sea of *dhikr*,[1] kept afloat by various forms of dance.

---

1. Sufi (Islamic mystical) ritual of chanting, music, and even dance designed to heighten religious awareness.

Their recitations began with the calming, monotonous repetition of: "I put my trust in the One who is alive and never dies. I take refuge in the perfect words of God from the evil He created. I ask the forgiveness of God Almighty, who is the sole god, the Creator of the heavens and the earth and of everything between them, for all my crimes and misdeeds and for everything I have inflicted on myself."

Shortly thereafter, the voices of the men in the circle gradually grew louder and the beat of the words became more pronounced:

> The Mighty who is exalted, there is no god but God,
> The Wise who is beautiful, there is no god but God,
> The Great who is perfect, there is no god but God,
> The Proximate who is gracious, there is no god but God,
> The Responsive who is righteous, there is no god but God,
> The Merciful who is benevolent, there is no god but God.

Then, suddenly, the Sufi Master stood up, and everyone in the circle rose. Roaring as loudly as they could, they made a noise like an earthquake. At the same time the doors and windows were closed, and the shrine was thrown into utter darkness. Voices quavered and grew louder. The world began to swell and heave as people's heads started to roll on their shoulders and bodies began to tremble, rising from the floor and sinking back. Feet felt tired, and the men's *jebbas* flapped open and closed as the circle rose and fell. Their warm bodies pressed together and then separated, scraping against each other and trembling, flowing with sweat, pressing, and yearning passion-

ately, while the phantoms of the women, who were dancing along with the rest of the congregation, were visible in
their enclosures through a diaphanous curtain. Liberated
from their scarves, their hair flew free and tossed about, as
they rose and squatted, scrambling up from the floor and
sinking back down in a crush of quivering bodies. From
time to time, the shrill but stifled shriek of a wounded soul
was heard as someone cried out and then fell into a swoon.
The Sufi chants continued to a monotonous beat, but the
dancing was bizarre and strange.

> O King, O Holy, Mighty, Omnipotent One,
> Glorified One, Holy, Mighty, Omnipotent One,
> Eternally Existent One, Mighty God,
> Potent Sovereign, Mighty God,
> Vanquisher, Mighty God,
> Wise Witness, Mighty God,
> Wise Omniscient, Mighty God,
> All-Hearing, All-Seeing, Mighty God,
> Gracious Omniscient, Mighty God.

Zuhra's clever subterfuge, through which Murtada had
escaped punishment, the way he had supported her by
pretending to go crazy too, his previous experiences with
Salih al-Fayyash, including the lie the boy had devised to
trick him and the pains Murtada suffered the night they
searched for treasure, not to mention everything he had
lived through and endured, all those preceding events and
the circumstances: these would have sufficed to transform
him into a pseudo-dervish and a skilled Qur'an reciter for
the souls of the dead. They eventually led him to this

shrine, that of Sidi Bin Isa, where he plunged with other surfers into the Sufi *dhikr* recitations and swam with them through their dances.

Murtada watched what was going on around him, feeling hotter than a burning coal. He eagerly anticipated the end of all this, so he could escape outdoors to the wide-open spaces where there was sunshine. Then he would flee far, far away from all these forms of mummery.

9

Uncle Mansur was astonishingly different from other members of the family. You could sense a hidden strength in his glances and an obstinate determination in his footsteps. When he spoke, it was with confidence for the future, no matter how cowed he seemed, for behind a submissive facade he hid a resolve that could demolish mountains.

When his daughter Zuhra entered his room as usual one day to clean and tidy it and to see to his needs, her father told her, "You don't need to go to that shrine. It won't cure you. Avoid provocations, and you'll heal yourself."

Zuhra answered, "But I'll take Murtada to the shrine of Sidi Bin Isa."

"You and Murtada are coming on an excursion with me. I'm taking you both to your uncle al-Hadi's house." Murtada returned happy from that outing. For the first time he had passed a Friday without feeling morose.

Uncle Mansur changed jobs frequently, moving from

the railway company to a tobacco warehouse and fuel depot and, after that, to a position as a doorman at postal headquarters. He worked in many different places, performing all sorts of tasks, and did his compulsory military service in the French armed services. Afterward, he fought an uphill battle with the vicissitudes of life. No sooner would he settle down in a position than he would leave it, for one reason or another. He hated all forms of oppression and rebelled against the despotic regulations that granted French citizens special privileges while handicapping Tunisians and shackling them.

Each time he was dismissed from a job, whether for trade union activities, for membership in UGTT, the Tunisian General Labor Union, for zealous attendance at meetings held at the Union's headquarters in Sidi Ali Azzuz Square, or for hanging on every word spoken by the labor leader Farhat Hached, he declared, " 'We must charge into the fray, which is entering its decisive phase. The hour of liberation is coming: there's no doubt about that. It will be achieved only through patience, endurance, and firmness,' as the leader said."

Reverberating calmly and evenly, Uncle Mansur's voice seemed to reach you from a distance, even if he was nearby. When you were with him, you felt at ease and at peace. He provided you with affection and love, which were palpable in his easygoing manner, graceful gestures, and tender words. He would listen to you, understand you, and delight you with entertaining stories and sweet songs. When he was in the armed services, he normally began with this poem:

[I'm spending] two years as an exile in a camp,
My head heavy with burdens;
The sergeant's yelling at me.
The beast's deprived me of my sleep.
Lord, make life easier for me
And arrange my discharge.

Then he would start singing his favorite song:

I was patient for two years for my country's sake, two years.
I was patient for two years; with laughing mouth but weeping
    heart;
For my country, I was patient for two years.
First off they gave me an aluminum cup and a spoon.
Then they placed a bit of bread in front of me and served me
    soup in a tiny bowl.
For my country, I was patient for two years:
They made us stand in lines so long I couldn't walk straight.
A man of swinish pleasures glared at me with an eye that
    scorched me,
An eye that scorched me. Sneaking up on me,
He raised his palm threateningly and then struck me.
I said: Lord, where can I flee?
For my country, I was patient for two years.

When Uncle Mansur reached this refrain, he would start sobbing. Every time he sang this song, he wept when he reached this phrase. He would weep and hold his hands high to express his disapproval and protest. He would curse colonialism and the tyranny it brought and vow to combat it and to evict the colonial power from his homeland. Then he would continue with the rest of the song:

Greet my family for me
And anyone who asks about me.
You'll reach our house if you go by the eastern side of town.
You will reach our house and then
You must tell my mother that
While I live, I'll return to her.
Some of the days have already passed.
For my country, I'll be patient for two years
For my country!

He would say, "These colonialists aren't strong enough to keep us from rebelling. We can rebel against anything. There is nothing, no matter how big or great, that should render a man impotent. Hear that, Murtada?"

Murtada loved his uncle Mansur to distraction and awaited his return each day. When he saw him, he would race to him and then sit beside him to listen to his sweet songs and fascinating stories.

Once the boy saw him carry in a large picture, which he hung on the wall in a prominent position. Murtada asked him, "Who's the man in that picture?"

"You'd like to know who the man in the picture is? My boy, this is Moncef Bey, the king who defended his people, who sacrificed himself for the glory of his nation, and who raised his voice to challenge the colonialists. He said, 'If I have to, I'll go down to Bab Souïka to lead the demonstrators. I want the first bullet fired to land in my chest. Then you can bury me in al-Jellaz, so I can stay as close to my people in death as I've been while alive.'

"The very first day he took the throne, he forbade people to kiss his hand, explaining, 'I don't want Tunisians humiliated in this way.' People loved him for that. He did not rule long, only for a few months, but this period was filled with events and tribulations. It's a fact that great men's lives are judged not by their length but rather by their events: whether their deeds are of lasting significance.

"The colonial authorities deposed and exiled him: from Laghouat to Tinis, both in Algeria, and then to Pau in France. He remained there—as militant as ever, a firm believer in the right of his nation for freedom and independence—to the end of his days. Then they brought him home in a casket covered with the flag, and people came out to say farewell to their martyred king, carrying him on their shoulders in a national funeral procession to the cemetery of al-Jellaz, just as he had once requested, while they sang ballads and songs like this:

> A locomotive hurtling through the clouds,
> Parting the waters of life, and
> Brandishing aloft the glory of the nation:
> Sidi Moncef Bey.

From the labyrinths of the Dar al-Basha neighborhood, from the branching mazes of its alleys, rose the spirit of resistance. Citizens spilled from their homes as these demonstrations formed and as vast crowds assembled. Masses of people swept forth like a raging torrent, waving flags and shouting, "Freedom! Freedom! Freedom!"

The occupation forces were just as vehement. With heavy boots, they trampled the nation's soil. They peered into people's home with their blue eyes, their heads encased in helmets. They brandished their weapons in the nation's face and spread terror, fear, and devastation in the souls of its inhabitants. The soldiers fired in every direction, and the nation's children fell as martyrs, resisting these tyrannical soldiers. With their blood they cleansed Dar al-Basha's earth and the nation's.

The national struggle for independence from colonial rule flared up in every location, just as Uncle Mansur had hoped and wished. Occasionally he would spend the evening with other family members, and Tawfiq the son of Uncle al-Arabi would stop by to keep us company too. They would chat, give us the news, and discuss the building momentum of events.

News of the resistance movement flooded the cities and the countryside, spreading through villages and even nomadic communities. Workers launched a general strike, and demonstrations swept through the streets and squares. Older students started a hunger strike, and pupils in the lower grades left their classrooms to demonstrate in the streets.

Reports streamed in, from the north of the country and from south, east, and west: door-to-door searches, police raids on homes, evictions, and arrests, people tortured and many killed, the wounded wherever you looked. News reports arrived from the eastern regions including Beni Khallad, al-Ma'mura, Kelibiya, Hammamet, and Nabeul.

Then came the tragedy of Tazarka. When Uncle Mansur arrived that evening, he was uncharacteristically morose and depressed. With ashen face he sat, narrating the tragedy to us: "The sun was starting to set and had become a bright yellow, painting the horizon with tongues of flame. Farmers and workers were walking down narrow gullies in the fields on their way home, ripped by a chill winter wind. Their faces were splattered with dirt and their bodies soaked with the sweat after a hard day's labor dedicated to serving the earth. When they suddenly heard the roar of vehicles, they turned and saw a cloud of dust, spreading and rising in the air. In no time at all an army convoy consisting of tanks, transports, and machine guns appeared. As these drew nearer, the racket increased. Then the vehicles spread out and, in the wink of an eye, surrounded the small, peaceful village, which they approached from every side, attacking it.

"Hundreds of heavily armed soldiers descended ferociously on the village of Tazarka, spreading panic, death, and devastation. Terrified children ran to their mothers. Old men and women raced each other for their lives. Domestic animals—lambs, goats, horses, and donkeys—leapt past one another in alarm, and the poultry—chickens, geese, and turkeys—fluttered off in all directions. Reverberating gunshots resounded down the lanes. The tread of heavy military boots cowed the village.

"Soldiers raided the houses, ordered the unarmed men out of their homes and shops, and herded everyone into a square at the center of the village. There they aimed their rifles and submachine guns at the villagers, surrounding them from all sides and from the rooftops.

"Their commander produced a list of names of persons involved in the resistance movement and demanded that these individuals be produced on the spot. He threatened that if they were not, everyone in the village would be punished.

"The soldiers immediately started razing, demolishing, and destroying, and a series of explosions was heard from every direction. Tongues of flame reared up, smoke filled the air, and deafening gunfire was heard nonstop.

"Once it was dark, they took the men and shoved all of them into a single house, packing them inside. Then they locked the doors and set guards around it. Next they took the women away and assaulted them.

"The wretched men stayed awake all night, listening to the women's and girls' screams, which rang out in all directions. They shouted for help, but there was no one to answer their cries. Meanwhile the soldiers grew rowdy and laughed raucously. From time to time, a shot pierced the heart of the night.

"One of the villagers tried to break out of the house to defend his honor. He stormed the door, but they killed him. A second man tried, and they killed him . . . and a third.

"At dawn, a stillness settled over the village as the soldiers departed, followed by winds that blew them curses, for they left the village writhing in its disgrace. The local men went to investigate what had happened. It was only then that they realized how serious the disaster was, for the troops had raped the women, killing any who sought to defend her honor. The cowards had even slaughtered babies.

"They had terrified the children, tortured the old men, spoiled stocks of grain and oil, plundered the villagers' possessions, and stolen their livestock. They had demolished dwellings, set fire to huts, and razed the school.

"That convoy of soldiers departed, but after a few hours fresh troops arrived. They began to attack the village all over again: a new cast of soldiers come to replay the same tragedy using the identical script.

"They took turns attacking Tazarka for three whole days, keeping it under siege and making an example of its citizens, torturing them in many different ways."

At this point Uncle Mansur fell silent. Then he shook his head and looked up to the heavens with tear-filled eyes, his heart racked by pain and sorrow: "O night, O walls and sky, and you the land, mother of us all, O ancient community, Dar al-Basha and you, the children and grandchildren, tell each other—raising your voices to the skies—the calamities that befell the village of Tazarka and the pains it suffered at the hands of the new prince of torture. Ever since he learned to harness the energy of steam and to power machinery with it, he has held the whole world by the scruff of its neck. The colonial master exploits weak peoples, confiscates their land, deprives them of any possessions of value to their lives, strips them of their native attire, customs, traditions, manners, and language, and then unveils his vile face by committing the most atrocious and repulsive crimes against humanity."

Some days later, Uncle Mansur came home ashenfaced and unusually agitated one evening. He whispered to the family a few words that alarmed and disturbed them and brought looks of consternation to their faces. Next he grabbed some of his papers, placed them in a pot, poured kerosene over them, and set them on fire. Then he put a few of his belongings into a small valise, bade us all farewell, and departed.

Painful, distressing events followed each other in rapid

succession. Only a few days later, there was news that rocked people of the neighborhood: a report came that Uncle al-Arabi's son Tawfiq, while participating in a demonstration, had been felled by the bullet of a colonial soldier. He had died, sprawled out in pools of his own blood.

10

$\mathcal{M}$urtada took a short detour to pass by some of Dar al-Basha's more memorable structures, which peered down at him from idiosyncratic facades. These were the refined homes of the leading people of their age, and each had its own special characteristics and a distinctive allure. Some exuded a haughty, braggart arrogance, whereas others hinted at a deep sorrow. The gaudy paint on some made them seem circus performers, while others appeared weighed down with sorrows. None of them had been erected solely as an independent edifice. All were designed to fit into the prevailing order, to be in harmony with the area, to promote communication between people, and to provide a spectacle that animated life around them.

These windows were fraught with hidden treasures and secrets, and you loved to look up at them as you passed stealthily below, thinking that you might see Shama's face as she sat by the window.

Her jet-black hair, which was pulled away from her narrow, luminous forehead, was combed tight behind her ears, and knotted in the back as a braid into which silver threads were plaited. Shama would sit erect beside the embroidery frame, patiently moving her fingertips over the embroidery pattern, working the surface of the cloth as she embroidered her wedding dress with multicolored dotted circles, pearls, and jots and studded it with gemstones.

From time to time she would glance out the window—past the decorative ironwork grill and the stems of the carnations, jasmine, and jasminum sambac that climbed over a trellis on the balcony—to the street and the peddlers who happened by. Then a handsome youth passed beneath the window. She imagined it was her true love, and her heart pounded. Allowing needle and thread to drop from her fingers, she rested her cheek on the palm of her hand. She continued to watch this young man until he disappeared from sight. Then she blotted out all her surroundings and pictured herself a bride swaying forward in her embroidered, white wedding dress. Her father, al-Hajj al-Arabi al-Dabbagh, who was escorting her to her bridegroom's home, waved back the rows of wedding guests so she might pass between them. Her mother, her mother's closest friends, and the wedding hairdresser hovered around her, adjusting her dress. The band was playing lively airs, and censers were passed from hand to hand as many carefully blended mixtures of incense—*washaq, dad*, gum benzoin, and *qamari*—pervaded the air.[1] Trills of joy resounded. There was a vast assembly and twinkling lights. She was seated in front of everyone in her wedding

---

1. *Washaq, dad*, and *qamari* are all types of incense.

throne, which was decorated with a nuptial garland and bouquets of roses.

This time, there is no one at the window to watch for your arrival. You're not on your way to visit Shama. You have no date with her this evening. You won't find her waiting for you the way she did in former days. Back then, you would search for her face, and when you caught sight of her, you would stand awestruck in the street below. Then, her black eyes would flash with an enchanting, seductive sparkle, and a smile of delight would shimmer across her delicate, red lips, illuminating the gloomy recesses of your soul. An animating pulse would rush through your body as you plunged into a wave of agitated emotions and your blood caught fire.

Shama was the beautiful love who slipped surreptitiously into your life like a white lily growing in the midst of a tangle of wild grass and thorny weeds. You weren't ready to receive that love, for you had no background for it. All the same, something in her eyes beckoned you, and you could not resist or oppose it once you began stealing glances at her, hovering around her, concocting excuses to see her, and speaking with her. One day she responded by holding out her hand, and then you wanted to grasp it forever.

You found yourself drawn by a magical force to other lands, to a new world totally unlike Dar al-Basha. You wanted to end your confinement in Dar al-Basha and to break the chains that shackled you to this narrow world. You wanted to strike out far and wide, to venture through God's vast universe.

From the beginning, you realized that her path through life would differ from yours, since someone like you could never provide her with the happiness of which she dreamt or a jolly life like the one she led in the custody of her father, al-Hajj al-Arabi al-Dabbagh. You would gladly have sacrificed your life for her, groveled at her feet, or buried your head in her bosom, but the life you led was patently different and the path before you, which you would be compelled to travel, was beset by dangers. Worried that you would ruin her life, you fled. Something called you to travel far away. No matter how far you traveled, her face followed you, never leaving you for a moment. You dreamed of her when alone. You were feverish to contact her, but when she was before you, you did not know how to hold onto her. You always were like that: you could not hold onto anything beautiful that came your way. You forgot the people who loved you and abandoned any excellent thing to chase after everything foul. Then, afterward, you fell prey to despair and regret. All that remains of Shama is the moan rising from deep within you. You no longer know where she is or how time has dealt with her.

You left everything behind and went, alone, to cast yourself into the desert's inferno, where horses flee to run wild. You went there to find the horses, to search for them. You traveled a great distance and penetrated into the depths of the desert. You devised traps for them, blockaded them, and struggled with them. You captured them, but they escaped from you and fled. You captured them and they fled. You captured them, and they slipped away and fled. You captured them, and they slipped free and fled. You captured and captured and captured, and they fled and fled and fled, but you will keep on searching for them until you find them. You will capture those fugitive horses one day and then attempt to tame and train them. You will try to inoculate them against dread epidemics and deadly diseases.

You will search for them and search and search until you exhaust yourself and lose yourself in the desert, until news no longer reaches you. You will search for them until you tame them or die trying. The gleam of yearning will sparkle in the heaven of their distant faces. You will stretch out your parched, trembling fingers to beg them for deliverance. You will clutch them avidly, wishing to press as hard as possible. The blood will course through your veins ever more intensely, and you will press forward across the sands with the last of your failing powers and all the strength your sick body can muster.

Blaze forth, you fires that spring from the depths of the desert, blaze as ardently as my heart. Blaze forth in a blind fury, striking wherever you wish—without repose or respite—and then warm yourself by the fires of hell.

The red dust is the color of the blood flowing from your old wound. The recalcitrant phrase catches halfway up your throat. Just thinking about dying makes you feel that you are. You will be twice a coward and doubly contemptible if you do not confront things as you should. How much longer will you persist in keeping secret what you should say and in blurting out what you should conceal? The truth does not require all this cunning.

For how much longer will you remain nailed to his doorposts, while he glares at you through his glassy orbs?

Move away from those looks that scatter sparks of hatred and rancor. Ever since you learned to despise those glassy eyes that ruined your life with the limitations they imposed on you and the obstacles they placed in your path, you have struggled until you were finally able to liberate yourself from the force of his tyranny so that nothing held you fast to his doorposts any longer. Everything connecting the two of you disappeared, and you did not even remember his tired, scowling face. The vast desert separated you. Cursed be the days you knew him and cursed be you if you start to brood about them again. You need to press your wine from vines you have planted yourself. Your mother did not wrap you at birth in woolens in hopes you would be afraid of stumbling later on. You tried so hard to fall, your feet became clumsy. Your night and life dragged on. Many of those who stood in line in front of you collapsed, but despair did not creep into your eyes. You confronted many harsh trials: you slept on the thresholds of warehouses, on the street through severe winter nights, you were buffeted by winds strong enough to demolish the portals of towering palaces, and bitterness devastated your heart. You survived all that without ever admitting defeat. You did not spend long periods thumbing through yellow-paged books, with margins crammed with commentaries, so that you would cringe at the changing prospects of this transient life.

11

*Y*ou have reached Ramadan Bey Square, which although small, suddenly widens to surprise us, flowing out in all directions like light eclipsing darkness. Many roads branch off from it, and Pasha Street ends there after a prolonged circuit.

There are mazes of little streets to the right and left: Ben Najma Street, al-Agha Street, al-Maqta' Street, Waterwheel Street, al-Qalash Street, Sidi Ibrahim al-Rayyahi Street, al-Kahiya Street, and Gharnuta Street. These tiny lanes widen, only to narrow again. Some lead into others, and a person strolling through this neighborhood will easily lose his way, because of all the twists and turns.

You wish you could hug some of the places, since they are near to your heart, however remote they seem. There are sunlit spaces, shady ones, brilliant colors, dark hues, and scenes of a lively and inspiring type.

Even so, I always dreamed of running away from here and leaving home. I don't remember where I got this idea or how it slipped into my consciousness. No matter how many times I tried to distance myself from it, I found it pursuing me, dogging my steps, and clinging to me, swelling ever huger in my head with each new tyranny and pain I suffered and with the passing days. It overwhelmed me until I was no longer able to free myself from it.

Fleeing far away became one of my fondest wishes, no matter what happened then. I would work as a shepherd, tending flocks of sheep and other livestock in distant pastures. I would scale lofty mountain peaks while inhaling the fragrance of wormwood, rosemary, and thyme. I would work as a farm laborer, tilling the earth on some remote estate. I would wander through wild lands. I would enter the trackless desert for an unknown destination.

The important thing was to escape from this house, from the glare of those humorless eyes, from all those people who were so busy with their private affairs that they had no time for you, leaving you feeling invisible. When they did crowd around you, all you heard was scolding and rebukes.

This idea of running away from home may have originated that first day when the woman took my hand—after my mother had entrusted me to her—and led me to Dar al-Basha. The moment I sensed the conspiracy they had hatched against me, I tried to wrest my hand free of that woman's grip, and my fingers fluttered like the wings of a sparrow wanting to fly off. But where could he go? She grasped him tightly.

That was a childish protest, and furtive at that. It was followed by another idiotic escape attempt that left me with a bitter taste and was eventually forgotten. When I was about ten, I gathered some of my clothes one day and headed for the house where I had last seen my mother, in al-Hafir Street. When I entered, everyone stared at me incredulously: "What's this boy doing here?"

Their confusion was obvious, and their faces betrayed disbelief and anxiety, despite the trouble to which Zaynab, the eldest of my female cousins, went to welcome me and make me feel at ease. Busy with their own problems, they were not ready to assume this kind of burden that did not concern them. I felt a searing pain in my gut and deeply regretted what I had done.

When I asked about my mother, they said, "Your mother's no longer here. She married and moved away long ago."

Then they wasted no time in pressing my clothes back into my hand and showing me to the door. So I returned home, devastated by this disappointment.

That chilling blow struck home, and I said nothing about it. Years that scarred me as deeply and mercilessly as a knife passed while I went back and forth between the Qur'an school and the Qur'anic recitation groups at ez-Zitouna Mosque. Any free time or days off I had I spent working.

I started in the souk of the *sheshya* makers as an apprentice to Uncle Hamada, who recited the Qur'an with us at ez-Zitouna Mosque. Once a week he would climb the minaret to give the call to prayer. He had a strong, musical voice. I climbed the minaret with him one time, and when I heard him summon people to prayer, my heart was convulsed with fear. When I began working in his shop as an apprentice, I discovered that he had an excellent singing voice too. While he worked, he would sing.

I stayed in this shop for quite a while. I observed and watched. Finally I took the *dabnina* in my hand,[1] climbed on the bench, and started to work.

There, in Uncle Hamada's shop, I discovered the stages in the production of the *sheshya* cap. It begins with spinning the right kind of wool thread for the *sheshya*. This job is the province of Tunisian women, who perform it at home. Then it passes to firms that wash and stretch the wool. Then the wool is subjected to the carding process and sent off again, to the dye works, before returning once more to the souk, where delicate tasks—like carding the wool between two paddles—are performed. Then the wool is placed in the mold to form the *sheshya*. Next there is the "beating" process to soften the fibers before it is sent once more to the women who adorn each cap at home, placing the firm's label inside. This task is typically performed by women.

Each of these complicated stages in the production— all this activity, and all this energy, and all the establishments and craftsmen associated with these processes, the tools they used, the means of distribution, and the inevitable interchanges between the craftsmen and the retailers—centered on the souk of the *sheshya* makers.

The future of this souk, where activity was starting to wane, was uncertain, and the market was stagnant, be-

---

1. A *dabnina* is a tool for softening a *sheshya* after it has been formed but before it is dyed.

cause, increasingly, people were abandoning the *sheshya*. The artisans had begun drifting away with the changing times, searching for alternative crafts and locking the doors of their shops. My father was an exception, for he insisted that I always wear a *sheshya*. His obstinate insistence on this strained one's credulity. The *sheshya* appeared to be absolutely the only thing that mattered about me. He did not insist on this out of any concern for my head's well-being. The point was, rather, to impose his will. He wanted it clear that his word was all that counted, even when his demand ran counter to prevailing fashions and trends.

I did not stay in this craft long. I transferred then to a tailor's shop in Sidi Bin Arus Street. This establishment was entirely different, for it teemed with activity and liveliness. It was so crowded with people, events, and history that it resembled a school. I learned much there, but some things escaped me.

Mr. al-Tayyib, the owner of the shop, was a person of many talents and had a finger in many pies. He was a master of genteel tailoring and was highly skilled in cutting out garments, performing this task himself. He ran the establishment and watched vigilantly over the concerns of his employees, who were of many different types, ethnic backgrounds, and ages. You would find workers there who were Jewish or Italian, young or old, and educated or uneducated. There was even one who could not speak. In addition to managing the shop, Mr. al-Tayyib had many other public interests and participated enthusiastically in other vital domains of the nation's life.

He worked earnestly and determinedly for the welfare

of Tunisian young people and was one of the founders of many of the athletic associations in the country, such as the African Club Association and al-Zaytuna Athletic Club. He was also head of the North African Track and Field Conference, and of the Tunisian Conference as well. He was the spirit of fitness recreation and its throbbing heart. He was a commercial powerhouse too, since he was a member of the Tunisian Chamber of Commerce and a director of the Tailors' Guild.

He balanced all these different responsibilities and met each with firm determination. He was very modest but self-confident. A man of noble and refined sentiments, he dedicated himself wholeheartedly to his work and allotted to each endeavor an appropriate effort. He revered nothing so much in life as the truth.

His opposition to colonial exploitation had earned him deportation and punishment, but he remained steadfast and defiant. He loved his country and was ready to sacrifice everything he held dear for its sake. Thanks to his diverse activities, he welcomed in his shop a variety of people, including well-known figures in Tunisian society. He entertained politicians, sportsmen, poets, actors, and musicians.

I once saw the poet Munawwir Samadih there, and I worked side by side with the musician and songwriter Ahmad al-Qala'i. Back then, the latter would bring his lute with him and occasionally play for us and sing us some songs of Abd al-Wahhab. One day the nationalist leader Habib Bourguiba came to the store. He parked his red convertible in Ramadan Bey Square and came to visit Mr. al-Tayyib, whom he engaged in conversation. He would joke around with our boss and call him "Egghead." All his friends teased him and called him this.

Mr. al-Tayyib truly was an egghead, for everything about him bespoke dignity and composure but, equally, benevolence and generosity. Full-faced and fair-skinned, he welcomed his visitors with a friendly smile. He carried his swelling belly in front of him, compressed into his new suit. His fez was pushed back a bit on his head and his jacket was always unbuttoned, because he had a habit of groping about in the pocket of his vest as if to signify to the person with whom he was speaking, "Sorry, I've let you down."

Mr. al-Tayyib, despite commercial pressures, his work-load, the many problems he faced, and the diversity of his employees and their occasional quarrels, dealt effectively with problems and imposed his authority, calmly and intelligently, by the sheer force of his personality. When he returned to the shop, his appearance at the door would immediately suffice to restore order, and everyone would return to work.

His tailor shop swarmed like a beehive with workers, their numbers increasing or decreasing in response to the firm's needs and the demands of a particular contract Mr. al-Tayyib had signed with a government agency to supply uniforms—for postal workers one time, for customs agents another—and for other types of garments. The work changed according to the seasons and the variety of garment appropriate to each. Once winter clothing was finished, summer clothes went into production, and so on throughout the year.

Mr. al-Tayyib's multiple interests and his frequent pre-

occupation with duties outside the shop gradually allowed
Master Tailor Abd al-Wahhab to take over supervision of
the workers and management of the firm. He was a young
man in the prime of life, throbbing with vitality and over-
flowing with activity and energy. He was a master of his
craft, and this was especially evident when he stood behind the cutting table, scissors in hand. This was the most
delicate and demanding operation upon which all the
other stages of production depended. The way a garment
was cut determined its characteristics; any mistake in this
process could easily spoil the garment.

Master Abd al-Wahhab was tall and graceful. His hair
was thick and black, and he had a gold tooth that glistened when he laughed or spoke. He was quite conceited,
especially once the star of his talent began to shine in art's
firmament, for in addition to his numerous other talents
he was an actor. One of the Tunisian theater's grand old
men, an actor who frequented the shop, taught him to
love this art and encouraged him to try it. So he appeared
on stage, even though he never became famous.

Since Master Abd al-Wahhab worked a lot, he was
concerned with his health. Therefore, he would send me
each morning from Sidi Bin Arus Street all the way to the
far end of the neighborhood of al-Hafsiya to bring him
back two egg yolks, which I would transport in two cups
after the vendor had drained off the egg whites, leaving
me half a shell for each. I would cover this entire distance,
panting for breath, fixated on the motion of the two yolks
that jiggled about in my hand for fear they would spill
onto the street, while passersby stared at my cargo. I won-
dered why he did not buy the egg whole and break it him-

self. Was the process of breaking an egg and extracting the yolk so difficult that it was worth all this effort? Did that vendor possess some exceptional gift? I do not know. This errand remains a mystery I still don't understand.

He loved women to an insane degree, and his eyes were always wandering to the street to follow some woman's silhouette. Sometimes he would drop what he was working on and run outside to chase after a woman passing there. He would disappear for a time of uncertain duration before returning.

Eventually, he started arranging dates with them inside our shop. They would arrive all wrapped up in veils and stoles and enter the woman's area. He would pull the curtain down behind them, in plain view of all the workers. He became so daring that he did this once when Mr. al-Tayyib was present, before his very eyes. He brought in one of these veiled beauties as usual and pulled the curtain down behind her. A terrifying silence reigned as every eye turned toward Mr. al-Tayyib. All he did was to stand up, don his suit coat, and leave the shop without so much as a whisper.

The only man to oppose Abd al-Wahhab or to criticize him for what he was doing was Master Tailor Lalo, who was the oldest of all the employees. From where he sat behind a sewing machine he stared at Abd al-Wahhab through glasses that slipped down the bridge of his nose and said calmly, "What you have done is inappropriate. It is very, very, very wrong." He did not elaborate.

The shop usually employed six master tailors, give or take a couple. We boys at the apprentice stage were affiliated with one of the master tailors and called him "my master." We would receive our orders from him and work under his supervision and guidance, although we could switch masters without any fuss. During the years I spent in this establishment, I was able to change from one master tailor to another.

My first master was Quba'a, who gazed at me from a long, brown face with a scar at the bottom of his cheek where his beard would not grow and told me: "Hold out your right hand."

I held my hand out to him, and he began to examine it between both of his. Then he grasped my middle finger and started to bend it and then stretch it back. He said, "Now I'll break your finger for you."

I pulled my hand away and looked at him incredulously. He smiled at me and explained, "I see you're upset. If you want to become a tailor, we'll have to break your finger. That's necessary for anyone who wants to learn this craft, so you can slip the thimble on your finger." Holding out his hand to me, he continued: "Look at my finger: see how easily I can bend it. Can you do that? Of course you can't. Don't be alarmed. It's no big deal."

He took a small strip of cloth, bent my middle finger, and bound it tight with this strip. Then he began to instruct me in the secrets of the craft. Each trade has its secrets, which we could spend a lifetime trying to discover. Perhaps we grasp them only after it is too late. At any rate, we never did discover the secret behind this operation to bend the finger. Then he began to issue me a list of do's and don'ts: "Do it like this, not like that." I quickly realized, however, that this was merely an approach he used to ingratiate himself with you, so that you would feel dependent on him.

Quba'a worked like ox all the time and was unusually forbearing. Master Abd al-Wahhab used to tease him in crude ways, setting traps for him and allowing sarcasm to escalate into humiliation and debasement. One time, he began as usual to speak rudely to him, alleging untrue things about him, but Quba'a's self-defense was so witty that everyone laughed. Master Abd al-Wahhab could not stand this triumph. He went up to the man and shoved him roughly, wanting to spit in his mouth. There was a violent struggle, which ended only when Quba'a grudgingly admitted defeat. Master Abd al-Wahhab laughed so hard then that he collapsed. Meanwhile Quba'a was already back at work.

After Quba'a, I worked for Lalo, who would be calling for me all day long, since I was apt to slip off to joke around and have fun. He always wanted to see me beside him. He would send me to his wife in al-Hafsiya on some errand or other. Whenever I went to his house, I was repelled by the strong odor, which was a mixture of food smells and something else I never could pin down. His wife was always glad to see me. During the summer she would serve me carob-flavored syrup she poured into a cup with ice floating in it. Then I would go and play. When I eventually returned to the shop, I would find Lalo in an agitated state, especially if Master Abd al-Wahhab had asked for me and found me missing. Lalo would sweet-talk me into approaching him, pinch me hard on the thigh, and whisper to me, "Why did you take so long? My heart nearly broke, waiting for you. Why do you act like this every time we send you out on an errand? Why?"

At times I would not work for either of them but would shoo flies away from my other master, al-Nasir. I would grasp the flywhisk and stand at his feet to keep the flies off him. Master al-Nasir, who was the older brother of Master al-Tayyib, had a huge body afflicted by many ills. He was frequently absent. When he did come to the shop, they would place a commodious sofa in front of the cutting table, or occasionally behind it. He would sit there, stretching his legs out in front of him. He had sores all down the length of his legs, and these oozed with blood and pus. My mission was to stand before him and swat flies away, especially during the summer. If he had a visitor, he would release me from this task. The wife of the leader Habib Bourguiba would frequently visit us when her husband was in exile. She would chat for a time with my master, al-Nasir.

We youngsters had another job, that of transporting the garments once they reached a certain stage of completion to a Jewish seamstress who specialized in buttonholes. Every garment we made required these, and Jewish women performed this task. So you would see us, almost every day, going and coming to al-Hafsiya, carrying garments that were unfinished and returning with finished ones.

I liked for a boy named Farid, who worked with us, to accompany me on this mission. I would joke around with him and chat on the way, and each of us would spill his secrets to the other.

12

Farid was several years my senior. He was distinguished by his easygoing temperament and quick wit. When I was sent out to perform some errand for the firm, I would frequently delay my return to enjoy a show, play billiards, or roll dice. Whenever I got into hot water for this, Farid would devise a scheme to bail me out.

I felt a special fondness for him, and a strong friendship developed between us, so that we became almost inseparable. Even on days we didn't work, I would meet him and we would go places together. One time we would stroll through the Belvedere Gardens, and another time we would see a film. He was in love with a girl named Su'ad who lived near their house, and he would always tell me about her. I was in love with a girl named Shama, who lived near us, and I was always telling him about her. He would frequently repeat her name, "Su'ad, Su'ad, Su'ad," and cry out, "I love her, Murtada. Do you hear? I love her!"

I would repeat the name Shama and tell Farid, "I love her, but I don't expect you to listen to me, because there's no hope of that."

Once, by chance, we witnessed a romantic tryst. We joked and talked about it for a long time afterward. That day, after we had carried garments to al-Uyun, Farid and I had the bright idea of climbing to the building's flat roof to see what the city looked like from that high up. We leaned over the stone railing there, supporting ourselves on our elbows. Facing us, but at a lower level, a woman was standing at a window. We positioned ourselves where we could watch her without her seeing us. Then we saw a man approach her, take her in his arms, and pull her toward him. He started caressing her and encountered no resistance or disapproval from her. Next he stretched out his hand and stroked her rounded bottom. He passed his arms under hers and pressed her swelling bosom tight against him, while she stood there submissively. Then he took possession of her mouth, as his lips seized hold of hers. Finally he drew her back into the room, and we lost sight of them.

We, in turn, stepped back from the stone railing on which we had been leaning. Then, all at once, for no apparent reason, we fled at top speed, as if someone were chasing us. We leapt down the stairs, almost flying, and descended three floors in the wink of an eye. We charged out into the street, galloping blindly, until we were out of breath and had to stop. Then we began to laugh. We laughed and laughed, until our eyes streamed with tears.

When Farid and I were together we would laugh at anything we encountered. Sometimes it was like that. At other times we would sit as quietly as hedgehogs rolled into a ball.

Whenever Farid swore by his mother's eternal life, I would immediately believe what he was saying, because

he loved his mother dearly. He would not swear to anything false when he mentioned her. His mother had died
when he was ten years old. He did not like his stepmother,
because she hated him and his father believed everything
she said. His father beat him all the time, and his home
life resembled mine. Like me, he was trying to think of a
way to run away from home.

We were walking along one day when we saw a vehicle
that was loading travelers, who were saying farewell to
their relatives. They were kissing each other good-bye,
apparently preparing to travel far away. Farid sighed and
commented, "Oh! If only I were leaving with them!"

From the very depths of my being I cried out, "I'd give
anything to travel far away."

Farid asked me, "Have you been thinking about that?"

"For a long time."

"Me too: I'd love to travel."

"Why don't we travel together?"

"But where?"

"Any place in the world."

"Do you really mean that?"

"It's what I've always dreamed of."

"What will we do when we get there?"

"Anything. What's important is gaining our freedom."

Farid's eyes shone with the most luminous smile I had
ever seen in my whole life when he heard this expression:
our freedom. I wheeled around and slapped my hand
down on his. He squeezed my hand and I squeezed back
hard. We shouted in unison, "It's a deal! We agree!"

We floated in our fantasy for a time. Then, turning toward me, he said, "But don't tell anyone."

"Don't tell anyone, yourself, either."

After that, we sank into silence, and then each of us went back to work. I was overwhelmed by a profound melancholy. Days passed without me touching my food. We saw each other in the shop but did not have an opportunity to talk. When we eventually did meet, I asked Farid, "Are you still as ready as I am to do what we agreed on?"

"I'm still ready, but I've thought of something."

"What have you thought of?"

"What would you say to joining the armed services?"

"I'd never thought of that."

"Would you want to?"

I hesitated for a moment. I thought of my grandfather and how he looked, erect in his military uniform, and of the strange things they recounted about him. I had never thought of following his path. Because of its rigor and restraints, army life had never appealed to me. I would have preferred a more remote destination that offered more freedom, but what could I do when there was no other way to escape? So I agreed and asked Farid, "What do we need to do?"

"We write letters asking to enlist in the navy in Ferryville."

We sat down, and Farid composed the letters, to which we attached our birth certificates. We waited for the reply with passionate concern. After a short time, Farid received a positive response and was transported by joy. In my letter, they apologized that I had not yet reached the age of enlistment.

After Farid departed, I quit the tailor shop. I felt I was

growing up and that this trade no longer appealed to me, for it required sharp eyes to thread a needle and to place the stitches neatly beside each other, uniting wool to silk. I was nearsighted and did not like the idea of wearing glasses. Tailoring is hard on the eyes, and I wanted to preserve my eyesight for whatever other tasks awaited me in future days, like reading books.

13

During the celebration of Laylat al-Qadr, the Bey made an appearance at ez-Zitouna Mosque and visited the souks of the old city. As the magnificent procession traversed Pasha Street, the Bey could be seen in a carriage drawn by six superb horses and surrounded by a troupe of cavalrymen brandishing swords. He sat proudly in his heavy ceremonial uniform. Medals covered his chest and dangled from his neck, and a mauve crown ornamented with gold sat atop his head. His thick black beard was streaked with gray, and his long mustache was twisted at the ends. From time to time he looked down over the crowds massed on either side of the street and nodded his head in a dignified fashion, but without a smile.

During public celebrations and festivities of this kind, Pasha Street was crowded with groups from various different Sufi fraternities. The Qadiriya delegation appeared with a throng of spiritual guides and their disciples, who were preceded by rows of red, green, and black flags and banners. At the head of the procession was the order's shaykh, who was followed by its disciplinarian or Bash Shaoush, mendicant Sufis, and then the order's standard-bearer. Next came disciples bearing ritual litters on their shoulders or carrying spears, candelabra, censers, incense pots, and goblets. Some played little kettledrums, large flat frame drums, or tambourines, while their cries resounded: "O Master Abd al-Qadir! O Bu Darbala! O Sultan of the city!"

Salih al-Fayyash caught sight of me as our paths crossed. He immediately seized me, squeezing me with both hands, and shoved me into the middle of the procession. He was in an intoxicated trance, and I did not want to spoil his altered consciousness by protesting. His *jebba* was shaking and seemed ready to fall from his shoulders. He was lunging back and forth with the others and trying to keep people in lines, going and coming, shouting and crying out, "O Master Abd al-Qadir! O Sultan of the Righteous!"

He was overtaken by a state of ecstasy that reflected off everything around him. Its sway over him was prolonged and submerged the souls of those near him. Eventually it encompassed the surrounding walls, doors, arches, windows, all the lights and shadows, and finally the earth and the sky.

For the first time in my life, I found myself abandoning my natural, obstinate reserve and surrendering to the current that drove me along with it. My thinking ceased as colors wove themselves into patterns before my eyes to form evolving images. I imagined myself riding on the back of a dream. Intoxication caused me to soar into the

unknown, carrying me high up toward vast horizons, as
the sound of the chant rose:

> I called out in the middle of the night,
> While my heart, wild with love, was yearning:
> Why are you so slow, Abu Jalul,
> To show yourself to your devoted lover who cries out?

The street before me shone with a splendid light, and I
pressed forward, surrounded by other delirious lost souls
like myself, until I was an arm's length or less from the sub-
lime shrine. I found it surrounded by people who were
stalled at its thresholds. They waited at its portals until
they could attain the light of truth and attempt to advance up the fraternity's spiritual hierarchy. I remained
stalled with the rest of them and waited for my turn like
the others. Finally I crossed the threshold and entered the
shrine with a pure heart, trembling and tumbling forward
under the influence of the chant:

> We twist a turban from water
> And tilt it slightly to one side;
> We make from ice a flaming lamp,
> When our chants' fiery waves collide.

Entering places like these is no easy matter; it requires patience through long periods and refined passion. Moreover, there are special steps: paths to be followed and rites
to be practiced, if one desires to sit with the Sufi circle or
to plunge into their spiritual floods, swim in their seas,
and probe their depths, in order, one day, to discover their

secrets and to attain what the masters of the Sufi spiritual states and of spiritual discipline have attained:

> Pay no attention as moons set and rise,
> We have a full moon that shames all others;
> From his brilliance, no matter what the hour,
> We have a light that the passing eras cannot dim.

Then as the commotion around me increased, and the beat of the percussion instruments intensified, people started trying to shoulder each other aside, crowding forward. The kicks and blows grew stronger, and I was pushed ahead so roughly, in the center of this human flood, that I almost lost my footing and fell. The current was too strong for me to resist and swept me along with it.

As I contorted my body in an effort to reach heaven's secrets, something happened to awaken my anxiety. The stench from all these bodies was so stifling that I felt debilitated and almost passed out. The world became a blur. I fled from there as quickly as I could and sucked in the clean air. I found myself once again weighed down by doubts and anxiety.

I was fed up with myself, and the insignificance of my life was obvious to me. I considered my peers who went to government schools, carried schoolbags, and read books. They left school in clusters, chatting, debating, and laughing gleefully and wholeheartedly. I, on the other hand, found myself shackled by chains: the Qur'an school, the shop, and the Sufi recitation circles. I had memorized the Qur'an and relearned it again so thoroughly that numerous slates had been worn out in the

process. I had sat so long on the mat that my heels had become calloused. I had rubbed my fingers raw with the
moist clay when erasing the slates to start writing on them
again, even though at that time the Dar al-Basha neighborhood surrounding me was chock-a-block with secular
schools that cajoled, harassed, and seduced parents to en-
roll their children.

I realized that I was walking in an agitated manner,
trembling from fear, as crumpled and twisted as a white
paper catching fire. I was pursued by a terror that traversed
the walls and burrowed into my bones. It slipped into bed
with me when I rolled under the cover or whenever I was
alone.

I looked at the mirror and detested my appearance,
which seemed strange to me. I did not look like any of my
peers whom I encountered. I wore a red *sheshya* cap on my
head as if I were a soldier in the Bey's army. Without hesi-
tating for a moment, I ripped it off, tossing it far away, and
quit the house. Later, when I returned home, not thinking
about anything, I suddenly found him directly before me.
He cast me a terrifying glance that paralyzed me. I froze
where I stood, and then the blow struck home. I heard the
ringing of distant bells. I grasped at the wall. I felt I was
falling to the bottom of the abyss. My grandmother's room
was just ahead of me, and I fled into it, but a powerful kick
connected with me there. I was slammed forward. Staggering, I rocked into the large, high mirror with the huge
gilded frame. It fell from its towering height, creating
something like an earthquake. Bits and pieces of it flew in
every direction, and I heard my grandmother scream dis-

consolately, "You two fight, but I'm the one who pays the price!"

The eerie silence that is a disaster's aftermath reigned supreme. I saw him head toward me, very deliberately. What more could he want to do? Then he placed his hand on the pocket of my new vest, which I had sewn myself, and ripped it to shreds. For the first time in my life, I found myself looking up at him, for my fear had totally left me. I was healed from my malady. I gazed at him steadily, without saying a word. In his eyes I seemed to detect this message: "Perhaps you've become a man now."

I removed that torn vest and dropped it into the dead hedge. Then I walked out of the house with no thought of ever returning. I left our house and the Dar al-Basha neighborhood behind. I left behind me the firm walls, high portals, and closed windows, the Qur'an school, the slates, and the clay. I left behind me the Sufi recitation circles, their chants, and their dancing. I left behind me my traditions, customs, and heritage. I left behind me my honor and humiliation. I left behind me my wealth and poverty, my solace and sorrow, my comfort and affliction, my attire and fear. I left behind me my skin, love, name, life, and equilibrium. I lived forty years in a trackless wilderness, far from you, O Dar al-Basha.

The Final Quarter

♦ ♦ ♦

The Roar of Silence

14

$\mathcal{H}$ere is Murtada al-Shamikh coming in sight of his childhood home. He approaches it slowly. The scent of a bygone age assails his nostrils, and he feels animated by it. A fire courses through his veins, and memories are awakened. His breathing is as labored as an unrepentant lover's, and his heart pounds.

Why such haste? "The sun is racing toward" its "resting place,"[1] and he is stepping forward to knock on the door, without knowing who will open it. The door will stir his disbelief and astonishment when it swings open. How many treasures and marvels lie behind it? How many wounds and pains?

He cannot count the times his steps led him to this doorway when he was young, but on this occasion, his steps are different. He is face-to-face with the doorway and raises his eyes to it. Tiles with corroded decorations and ancient fish-scale patterns adorn the wall surrounding

---

1. Qur'an 36:38 (Ya Sin). The progress of the sun across the sky is a sign of God's transcendent power.

the portal. At the center is a high arch composed of de-
signs and shapes so worn that most of these decorations
have been obliterated. Only hints remain to provide the
facade with a leftover fragrance of his ancestors.

He lowers his gaze to the small, curved aperture at the
base of the grand doorway. How aged and deteriorated it
seems. Its rim slants painfully, leaving a gaping void like a
deep wound between it and the big door. Despite its dull,
faded color, and the gradual destruction that has marred
it, the little door, set within the larger one, still draws vitality from that grand door, which has continued to stand
strong in the face of time.

Without any hesitation, he steps forward and pushes
open the small door inset in the large one, just as he always did in the past, without knocking or waiting to see
who will open it. The little door emits a long, muffled
groan that echoes deep inside him.

He is not sure how he has actually managed to cross
the threshold and to enter the long, dark hall. Perhaps he
is driven ahead by old habits. Then he turns into the second hallway to emerge from it into the expansive courtyard paved with white marble set with decorative colored
inlays. This, too, is worn and cracked. There are many
gouges and scars in it, and dry grass has sprouted through
the fissures.

An aged tortoise slowly emerges from a basin housing
a barren palm, which grows in solitary splendor between
the four high walls of this space. The open sky is a source
of sunlight during the day, an arena for stars to glitter and
for the moon to release its glow once night falls, and space

for his spirit to reach out when feeling confined by the walls of a prison and for his thought to expand when hedged in on every side.

This is their home. Every door, corner, and black or white tile in it conveys some memory or some image— even if fleeting, intermingled, or interrupted—with agitated emotions and sweetness. Dead grass, a pot leaning on its side, a light green roof tile: melancholy and sympathy lurk everywhere.

His forefathers made this house hum with their fervent belief, good humor, toughness, and graciousness. Perhaps they possessed a great spiritual fortune, one that has resisted destruction. As he feels their qualities, the depth of the abyss separating the different ages is brought home to him.

The distant past was crowned with majesty. The recent past has been soiled by filth. Here's the present: gloomy to the edges, bounded by conspiracy.

Murtada al-Shamikh stands for a long time at the center of the house's courtyard without seeing anyone. He raises his voice to call, "People of the house, who's here? Isn't anyone home?"

In front of him, opposite the entry hall, is the salon with its domed roof. The door stands wide open. He heads there and crosses the threshold. Shafts of light reach down from the open window beneath the dome at the top of the ceiling. In the center of the room, beneath the dome, his father stands praying. Murtada recognizes him at first glance—the small frame and sturdy physique—although he seems slightly stooped and worn by time. He hears his father recite the Qur'anic verse:

When Moses came to the place We appointed, His Lord
spoke to him. He said, "Oh Lord, show Yourself so that I
may see You." He said, "You will never see Me, but cast
your eyes on the mountain. If it holds firm, you will see
me." When his Lord manifested Himself to the mountain, it was reduced to dust. Moses fainted. When he re-
gained consciousness, he said, "Glory to You. I turn to
You in repentance and I am the first of the believers." [2]

In a dazed state of homesickness, Murtada watches his
father bow, rise, and prostrate himself until he has finished
his prayers. Then without any hesitation, he says, "May
God accept your prayers, Father."

Rising from his prayer mat, his father turns toward
him, surprised by the voice. "Who's there?"

"Me, Murtada."

"Oh, so it's you. You've finally found your way home."

"How are you, Father?"

"Welcome."

The two men embrace, greeting one another like old
friends. Then his father begins to study Murtada through
thick glasses with eyes that still shoot forth those sparks,
but they seem less intense than before and rapidly change
into an affection that spreads out to traverse space and
time, encompassing the floor and the walls, the ceiling
and the domes, before they rise to the heavens and enter
the heart to instill love and mutual understanding. Invit-

---

2. Qur'an 7:143 (al-A'raf, meaning "the Heights"). The entire
verse is quoted here. The message is that even Moses, a prophet chosen
by God, is limited by his physicality in this life.

ing Murtada to sit beside him, he summons his new wife, who rushes in to stand before him.

Murtada looks at her in amazement. She is a middle-aged woman, brimming with vitality. He wonders privately what has become of the previous wife. Grasping his son's uncertainty, the old man clears up the matter: "The other one, after living with me for thirty years, changed on me, and so I let her go. She's probably living with her children. I'm old enough that I can't live alone." Then he introduces his new wife to Murtada before asking her to prepare supper for them. The two men sit talking together, choosing topics of general interest, without either of them touching on the past or recalling the circumstances that led to their separation and that caused Murtada to leave home and to remain estranged from it for all those long years. They chat as if nothing has happened, as if each knows everything about the other, as if they have never been separated for a day in their lives, and as if nothing has occurred to trouble their relationship.

Murtada stays with his father for some time. With a pained heart, he examines what the days have done to their house and what has become of it. Its condition has changed because of the long period of neglect. Agents of decay have crept through it, and age has whittled it down, so that it is on the verge of collapse. Murtada investigates the entire Dar al-Basha neighborhood. Houses that formerly were home to judges and to the city's most distinguished citizens and local notables have become rental tenements, inhabited by a motley crew with anarchic children everywhere, climbing the walls like columns of ants and filling the world with their uproar and quarrels. You see laundry lines strung any old place and nails pounded deep into each door and wall.

Murtada thinks about restoring the house and raises the matter with his father, who replies, "As for me, I've done my duty by it. I've preserved it intact to the present day. From now on, it's no longer my concern. It's your re-sponsibility, yours and your siblings' and your cousins'."

15

During the time that Dar al-Basha was collapsing, while its features were being obliterated and its importance was dwindling from one day to the next, other regions witnessed the birth of a new life and were transformed into dreadful proving grounds for both baseness and modernity.

The vast stretches of agricultural land and the lush gardens that once surrounded the city, acting as its lungs, became agglomerations of steel and reinforced concrete as apartment blocks crept everywhere, shooting up, crammed together like devils' heads. Villas were stacked beside each other like crates of vegetables, and tangled masses of streets twisted like the arms of an octopus. The way vehicles sped down the narrow, rutted streets, day and night, without interruption, was enough to make you faint. The city flowed out, oozing in every direction like fresh dough, to the north and the south, to the east and the west, in every possible direction.

Some districts will make your heart rejoice. They captivate you with their magic and beauty, their innovative structures, the geometrical clarity of their streets, and their carefully numbered houses, occupying streets each of which has a name. The identity of the residents is known, and they have registered deeds to their properties. They wear suits and drive cars. There are public gardens, playgrounds for their children, and designated parking lots. Street signs have been erected, and there are traffic signals, striped crosswalks for pedestrians, and clean sidewalks. You find fountains, glamour, and much more.

Most of the other areas are terrifying outlets for disorder and chaos. Styles clash there and are confounded. Residential units are heaped together and interspersed with factories. These areas lack the most basic amenities like sewers. Don't even ask about the rutted roads, the garbage strewn everywhere, the stench of open sewers, the swarming flies, dive-bombing mosquitoes, stray cats, or mad dogs. These areas are not villages with a village's serenity and beauty, nor are they cities at all comparable to a normal modern city.

An anxious generation confronts all this. Nervously and silently they observe all these indications of disorder and anarchy. They are at sea: torn between their upbringing at home, the principles and maxims they encounter at school, and the congestion, internecine strife, and decline of morals that they experience in daily life. Their sense of individual isolation increases every day, in step with their ongoing misfortunes.

It would seem that in olden days when people built their city and erected mosques, palaces, minarets, and domes, when they constructed houses and souks, raising walls and portals, they were self-confident and knew exactly what to do. They found ways to support themselves and to control the stages of production. Men and women were gainfully employed in agriculture, ceramics, textiles, and spinning wool. They worked side by side in rural areas and the cities. The artisan would undertake his craft with love and dexterity and perform it with extraordinary skill and talent. The result was a wealth of tools, styles, products for many different uses, and creative innovations of many different kinds.

This was an exuberant world of inner strength with boisterous activity and vibrant colors. People had a clear vision of life. They performed their necessary tasks in exactly the same way that they recited verses of the Qur'an. They understood and believed these intuitively and spontaneously, not wearing themselves out with exegesis.

People nowadays, however, do not know what they are doing. They plunder anything they can grab, whether antique or recent, from the East or the West. They speak every language. The clothing they wear comes from many different cities. They manipulate tools and instruments they have not themselves produced. They employ devices they have not helped invent. They spend money they do not possess, and they explain the meaning of the Qur'an however the spirit moves them. They adopt contradictory statutes, and they impose laws that they have not personally derived or drafted. They import everything, even freedom, the air they breathe, and the water they drink. They offer everything for sale to the highest bidder, from the produce of their fields to what lies beneath their skins.

They cannot distinguish one path from another and confuse everything so grievously that they mutilate the pattern of their city and disfigure its lands and structures.

What a distance separates the people of former times and our modern cities!

16

$\mathcal{M}$urtada al-Shamikh embarked on a whirlwind campaign, exploring the city and its far-flung extensions, traversing it from north to south and from east to west, in search of his siblings and cousins. As he inquired about them here and there, one long journey would propel him on an even longer one and each distant neighborhood would launch him toward another farther away. He struggled through a labyrinth of trains with their various routes, buses with all their different numbers and lines, and taxis of assorted sizes and colors.

In this city, where contacts had been abandoned, no one knew anyone else. No member of a family would think to ask about another family member or wonder how he was. At first, visits between families became fewer and less frequent, and family relationships weakened and grew lukewarm, until finally the day arrived when these visits ceased altogether. The distance between their homes, people's absorption in their own affairs, and their preoccupation with their jobs, which usurped most of their days and some of their evenings as well, all played a part in the disintegration of the extended family.

Each day Murtada al-Shamikh returned almost senseless from his excursions to the farthest reaches of the city. Exhausted by a feeling of helplessness, he was overwhelmed by utter despair. Among all those he contacted, he found no one interested in listening to him or ready to cooperate with him.

They would receive him with open arms, but the moment he began to talk about Dar al-Basha they would gaze at him incredulously and their faces would become large question marks, presaging derisive laughter and sarcasm.

The house in that ancient community no longer meant anything to them. The way they looked at him when he spoke excitedly about it showed that they harbored doubts concerning his sanity. He could see in their eyes their pity for him and their regret that he had fallen into such a condition. His final visit was to Mr. Nur al-Din, his uncle al-Hadi's son. He was a man of substance, with many responsibilities and enterprises. Murtada visited him at his office, where the man was quick to greet and welcome him, stepping out from behind his desk to sit in a chair facing Murtada's: "Please have a seat. What will you drink? Coffee?"

"Thank you. I don't care for anything. I won't take up much of your time."

"Please feel free to say what's on your mind."

"I've come with reference to our house in Dar al-Basha."

"Oh, the house in Dar al-Basha. . . . Whatever happened to it?"

"It's on the verge of collapse."

"You mean it hasn't collapsed yet?"

"It's an ancient landmark but needs some maintenance and repairs."

"I hope you'll believe me when I say that I'd forgotten its very existence. Since my late father moved out when we were young, I haven't heard anything about it or what had become of it."

"It's still standing but showing signs of its age, and the ravages of time have created some problems."

"What do you want?"

"For us to all pitch in to give it the care it requires."

"What kind of care?"

"Some structural repairs, for example."

"But the condition you describe makes it sound beyond repair. Because of the structural damage, it would require radical demolition to install new timbers. You might as well be asking for a heart transplant to bring a dead person back to life."

Murtada laughed to mask the pain he felt deep inside. "No, no, it's not that bad. The building doesn't require any demolition. Let's be more precise. This house was built hundreds of years ago. There's been some damage caused by wear and tear over the years. It needs some repairs—nothing more, nothing less."

"What do you expect from me?"

"To join with the other heirs to repair and renovate it."

Mr. Nur al-Din laughed so hard he could not sit up straight. Once he reclaimed his seat behind the desk—sitting erect—he cast Murtada an inquisitive glance across the broad desk, as if questioning the soundness of his mind. Then he asked, "Repair what? This house wants to fall down. Why don't we let it? That will be the end of the matter. These areas have died. They're finished. They no longer have a leg to stand on. They are as dead as my late father. Is he likely to return from the grave?"

"But it's your grandfather's house. You were born there."

"Listen, Mr. Murtada. The world has changed. People have stopped looking backward. That old house no longer has a role to play. It played its part, but that's over. It's not good for anything now—no way. People's lifestyles have changed. The way they live has, too. Their manner of thinking is different. That old house and all those old neighborhoods need to be torn down, so they can be re-built with structures that have the amenities that corre-spond to the requirements of modern life. The world is pushing forward. Anyone who continues to gaze behind him, at the past, will be left behind. He'll miss the train."

These ideas caught Murtada off guard. He did not want anyone to think he agreed with them, and he looked for ways to rebut them. He tried to remember a relevant Qur'anic verse, but to no avail. None came to mind, but some ideas surfaced from things he had read. He pro-ceeded to outline these: "Your steps as you advance into the future will be firmer if you glance back. For the future to be as firmly rooted as possible, the past must necessarily be reviewed. There can be no future, Mr. Nur al-Din, without a past."

"What past? The past befouled by dishonor and catas-trophes, the one based on exploitation and tyranny, on

slavery and the oppression of women, on the expropria-
tion of workers' rights, and on the denial of liberties?
These old neighborhoods, which you have come to defend, Mr. Murtada, were built on injustice. If we are to
root out tyranny and erase it from memory, we must sub-
stitute new neighborhoods for the old ones and expunge
them from our memory."

"Your memory seems to retain only the negative
things. You remember nothing of the bright moments or
positive advances."

"Perhaps we can preserve some of the palaces and
other buildings of artistic merit as a memento."

"So far as you're concerned, even radiant aspects of the
past seem nothing more than a spectacle, like a ballet presented on stage by a folkloric troupe, a performance of sa-
cred dance by disciples of Sidi Bin Isa, the Sufi processions
of the Qadiriya Brotherhood, or the craft of making a
sheshya cap. That's not really the past, Mr. Nur al-Din."

"What is the past then, according to you, Mr. Murtada?"

"The past is a spiritual strength and not the literal,
physical past."

"What spirit are you talking about?"

At this point, Murtada sensed that their conversation
was heading nowhere. He decided to change course, attempting to wrap up their discussion in his own fashion:
"The past is to repair your grandfather's house now."

"You want me to squander thousands of dinars on a de-
crepit old house that can never be brought up to code."

"But it's your grandfather's house where you were
born."

"I don't gamble recklessly with my money."

"You'll simply pay your share, like the other heirs."

"Have all the others agreed?"

"Only the majority need agree."

"I'll speak candidly. I'm not ready to throw away my money."

"That's your business." Then he suddenly felt like calling his cousin's bluff. So he added before the other man could reply, "Fine. Since you're not ready to help repair the house, are you prepared to renounce your share of this inheritance?"

Then Mr. Nur al-Din's stance altered, and his voice took on a ring of determination. "Why do you want me to renounce my rights to my grandfather's house?"

"Do you see how, deep inside, you're still attached to the past?"

"I always look ahead and think of the future."

"Since you look ahead, why not rid yourself of your share of the inheritance?"

"May God never deprive an heir of his due."

"What's to be done with you? You don't want to look after your inheritance and preserve it, but you refuse to wash your hands of it and renounce it. What do you call this?"

"I'll explain my views to you. Tracts of land surrounding the city used to be worth nothing, but now you see how their value has skyrocketed. Who knows? Perhaps Dar al-Basha's value will shoot up one day."

"Places don't have an intrinsic worth. We're the ones who assign them an appropriate value by the love we grant them, the work that we realize there, and the schemes that we devise. With our work—not with dreams—we can increase the value of Dar al-Basha."

At that point, Mr. Nur al-Din laughed out loud. He emerged from behind his desk to indicate that their conversation was over and declared, "My one fault is that I don't dream."

Murtada laughed along with his cousin as he took his leave at the door. "Dreams are beautiful," he said, "but work is even more beautiful."

17

At the end of Pasha Street you find a shrine dedicated to the memory of a holy man. Its portal hugs the line of facades of the neighboring buildings, and its window climbs the wall like a woman modestly averting her face. While children play in the street, men and white-clad women traverse it self-confidently. Their greetings follow a time-honored rhythm, either, "Good morning," or, in the evening, "Sleep tight," followed by:

"May God preserve you."

"May God bless you."

"May God assist you."

No one shuns another or raises his voice when speaking. Everyone here has been shaped into an ancient concord.

By the door of the mosque an old man supports himself with a stick. His *jebba* is shabby, and his beard is white. He holds out his hand: "Alms for God's sake, benevolent people. Alms for God."

You approach him and look attentively at him: you are

face-to-face with Salih al-Fayyash. Astonishment at fortune's reversals and fate's fickleness seizes you.

When Murtada returned home, he ate supper and then relaxed a bit. Next he started to prepare for bed. He may even have stretched out and slipped under the cover.

Suddenly he heard a thunderous noise that seemed to come from every direction, deafening him. He felt the earth rock under his feet. The walls split apart and crumpled. The ceiling broke away and collapsed in stacks. Then the rubble fell too, and shards of furniture were thrown about, strewn everywhere, and scattered. Murtada picked himself up only to tumble back down. Then the sky started falling on him. Chunks of dry dirt and stone poured over him where he lay. Afraid for his life, he put his hands over his head.

He lay in a stupor for a time, until the storm had passed. Then a profound silence like the tomb's smothered the place. He reached out a hand to wipe the dirt from his face. He raised his head, opened his eyes, and looked right and left, but darkness reigned everywhere. His head hurt and so did his left leg. He struggled to regain his composure and to fathom what had occurred. He said, "What a night! What's happened? Is it a bolt from heaven's wrath or has Dar al-Basha thrown down its burdens and vomited them up?"

He began to search for a way to escape from this scene of destruction. He shook the dust off and struggled to rise. He crept forward and then slithered on his belly, trying to get clear of the piles of dirt. He stretched out his arms to scout the area and to discover how much room he had to maneuver.

With considerable effort and difficulty, he freed himself from the piles of dirt and stones only to bump against a large, heavy rock over his head. He strained to push it away but merely exhausted himself. He abandoned this attempt and stretched a hand through the pitch-black gloom to feel around the rock. Discovering a large space beyond it, he poked his arm through. Although he moved it every which way, his arm came in contact with nothing. Hope dawned inside him and joy flooded him. He might be able to squeeze through this chokehold and emerge into the space on the far side.

He stuck out his head and flapped his arms the way the tortoise did from within her shell. Then he got his shoulders through that narrow gap and made a big, mindless surge ahead. There was still space before him. He pushed all his weight forward until he fell on the hard floor, on his head.

He rose to his feet and stretched his arms out before him. He began to grope about. He found that he could move freely in a space about a meter and a half deep. The area, which was blocked in every direction, was defined on one side by the corner of a room.

He started to scream at the top of his lungs, calling out. The sound of his voice returned to him from the depths of the darkness, its echo cycling back like the roar from the deep pit of a well. He picked up a stone and began to pound on the wall. He kept that up for some time and almost went insane (or perhaps he did become temporarily insane) until he was overcome by fatigue and collapsed in exhaustion. Then he halted while he put an ear to the wall to listen. Even though he waited for a long time, there was no sound of life. People and life in general seemed to have died as a whole, leaving only a silent void and darkness.

He calmed himself, realizing that if he continued in this anxious, tense state, he would certainly become debilitated and weak and rapidly break down. He thought he might be in for a lengthy stay in this pit under the rubble, a sojourn that might last days or possibly even weeks. He needed to husband his strength and conserve his powers for the days ahead.

In the deep gloom, he advised himself: "What's the use of yelling? There's no one there to hear your voice. You need to stay calm and conserve your energy for the coming days. You must be strong. What's required of you, Murtada, is to stay strong."

He remained standing, his face to the wall, his arms raised in front of him as if he had reached the point in his prayers when he glorified God. He took a deep breath and thanked God that he was still able to breathe. Sufficient air was able to reach him through crevices and nooks in the rubble and through gaps between the piles of rocks.

He was quiet for a moment. He put a hand on his chest and used it to monitor his heartbeats. He experimented with his breathing, inhaling deeply through his nostrils and filling his chest with air and then exhaling slowly through his mouth, releasing heavy, humid air that seemed to reek of the earth and of a mixture of other scents, of lime or rotting grass. He reflected: this is one of life's necessities. He had air to breathe. If he wanted to stay alive, he would need to procure water and food. Then he laughed, mocking himself: "Why am I thinking like this? It's not the right moment to think of such things." They were, quite possibly, at that very moment on their way to remove the thick covering from him and to pull him out of his distress. Moreover, he had eaten an excellent supper and drunk an adequate amount of water before retiring to bed. That should suffice while he resisted patiently for some time: days, perhaps weeks. He would have to set this matter aside and forget it.

Speaking aloud, he said, "You've got to forget this." He began to repeat the statement: "You've got to forget this. . . . You've got to forget this. . . . You've got to forget this. . . . You've got to forget it during your stay in this hole."

He was silent for a time. He remembered a verse from *Lamiyat al-Arab*[1] and repeated it silently: "I stave off my hunger so long I slay it; / I shun it so totally I forget it."[2]

He told himself again, aloud, "To be strong, you must first triumph over your self and dominate it. You must forget entirely about hunger and ignore it so thoroughly that you cease to remember it."

He thought about what he had said. Then he laughed sarcastically at his words. Silently this time, he chided himself: "You talk of triumph over self. Do you still have a self to conquer? For as long as you have had this self, they have been working to subdue, vanquish, humiliate, and destroy it. They taught you at home, in the Qur'an school, in the street, in the shop, at middle school, at ez-Zitouna

1. "Arab Poem Rhyming in the Letter L."
2. Al-Shanfara, *Lamiyat al-Arab*, 22. Al-Shanfara, a pre-Islamic Arab poet of the sixth century, is known for this poem and for affecting a Bedouin, outlaw stance.

Mosque, in books with yellowed pages, in new books, in newspapers, in magazines, from pulpits, in sermons, in public assemblies and in private discussions, in radio and television programs, in variety shows, in the songs you heard, in posters on walls, in directives, in movements, in glimpses, in whispers, and in malicious gossip: to curb your natural instinct to privilege your self. They instructed you to rein in your headstrong self, to resist your self, to vanquish your self, to humble your self, to devastate your self down to its core, and to triumph over your self.

"The poor self has borne everything and been patient, and now you finally have brought it to this nadir and made it crouch at the bottom of a pit, as low as possible, under this rubble. What greater conquest over self could there be than this?

"You triumphed over it until you neither laughed nor cried.

"You triumphed over it until you no longer felt joy or sorrow.

"You triumphed over it until you no longer experienced hunger or satiety.

"You triumphed over it until you were neither alive nor dead.

"What greater triumph than this could there be?

"You triumphed over it until you could no longer achieve victory or defeat.

"What greater triumph than this could there be?"

At this point, his internal discussion of the self ceased for a time. In a clear voice, he said aloud, "Even so, you must triumph over your self this time too and be patient.

You must be patient, and triumph, be patient and triumph, be patient and triumph, be patient and triumph. . ."

He stopped for a moment before adding in a louder voice: "Be patient and triumph, be patient and triumph, triumph and be patient, triumph and be patient, be patient and triumph, be patient and triumph and triumph and triumph and triumph and tr . . ."

He repeated this, time and again, wishing to experience the sound of his voice, since he had noticed a strange ring to it when it came back to him from the depths of the darkness. In this hole in the earth, below the rubble, it sounded like a roar rising from bottomless depths. He began to find this sound entertaining. He wanted to hear it again and again, more of it, each time he addressed himself out loud.

Perhaps he found in the echo of his voice some hint of companionship or human warmth to help ward off his feeling of isolation and loneliness. He began to vary his voice, speaking softly one time and then forcefully the next, sadly one time and gleefully the next, in a smooth and soft or trembling and quavering voice, until he felt exhausted. He was tired of hearing his own voice. He hated this self, despised it, and detested this loathsome game.

He was silent for a while. He felt a soothing tranquility encompass him and fill his being. He realized that he had been torturing himself by making all that racket. He had been providing an extra punishment for his self, over and above what had tumbled down on it from the heavens.

Feeling exasperated, he shouted, "What have I done, my Lord? What have I done to deserve this punishment?"

He was still for a moment. Then he asked, "What shall I do now? Yes, what should I do?"

He reflected: "How can I cope with all this? Indeed, how is it possible for someone like me to bear these burdens, to stand firm in the face of these trials for which I have never been prepared, which I have never been trained to withstand? Especially while I am in my present condition, weakened by my injuries but also suffering from chronic maladies and pains, with a crushed body and a broken spirit, antiquated cultural references, a language that has lost its purity through borrowings from others, eyes that have been dulled, and innumerable complexes derived from this old place, which is a deep-rooted world but in tatters. . ."

He was silent for some time as he peered about in the darkness. He asked, "How long have I been here?"

If he'd had his watch and lighter with him, he would be able to see the time, but he had nothing on him. He had been preparing to go to bed when fate devastated him and the building collapsed on him. He had nothing with him, certainly not a watch or a lighter.

So he asked himself, "What difference would it make if I knew the time? Does time have any intrinsic value in my circumstances? Let's suppose I knew the correct time right now, would that change my circumstances in any way?"

Time has no intrinsic value. It draws value from the movement and action that men create in it, from the work that man executes; that's what provides time with the meaning we seek to extract from it. Time has no existence independent of human activity.

Down through the various ages, whether in the Stone

Age or the ages following it, like the Bronze Age, the Iron Age, and down to the age of petroleum, only man has created time. Man alone, through his awe-inspiring cultural development has created these ages and constructed time with his diligence, thought, and genius, by the effort of his arm and the sweat of his brow.

"So long as I live in this hole, in suspended animation, I'll be living outside the circle of time and therefore outside of my era and my time.

"All my thought while I am in this hole under the rubble can be nothing more than mulling over what has been preserved from the past. I don't have access to the world of sight and can't pass judgment on that, and thus it's impossible for me to know what the future will be.

"The past has value when it's relevant to present human actions aimed at progress beyond this point, glancing ahead toward the future's horizons. When there is no human action or movement or liberty, there is no value to the past and no meaning to the future."

He told himself in a loud voice, "You must search for a way to get out of this impasse." Then he proceeded to investigate the area around him, feeling it, groping about with his fingers, familiarizing himself with it, discovering what it enclosed. He was in a cavelike area, a triangle with one right angle and two acute ones. In fact, one was so acute he could not even stick his hand all the way into it. The ceiling was falling, sinking down at an oblique angle that was frightening, given the ceiling's thickness.

He continued to grope about with his hands, avidly pursuing his investigations with the tips of his fingers, carefully studying every secret place, scrutinizing it, probing it, trying to push against it with all his strength, but to no avail. He found cavities, bulges, thick layers, rocks, and some areas that were darker than the rest.

It never occurred to him that the time might come when, although he lived on, the sun would not shine on him or that he would not see its light again.

He told himself in a calm, resolute voice, "Learn, Murtada. Learn how to live inside the grave. Learn how to endure in the depths of the tomb. Learn how to speak inside the tomb. Learn how to think within the catacombs. Learn how to listen to your soul's voice, how to convey the message to it, how to receive the message from it, how to preserve it without allowing it to perish, so you're never deprived of it."

He felt exhausted and slumped down. He sat on the floor at the deepest part of that hole. His hand touched the spot on his head where he had been hit. He discovered a viscous liquid on his fingers. Bringing his hand near his nose, he sniffed it and found that it smelled yeasty, like raw dough. His wound must still be bleeding. He had to stop this bleeding as quickly as possible, for he needed every drop of his blood.

He had never appreciated the value of his blood as acutely as he did now. He scooped up a handful of dirt and pressed it against his wound. Then he thought, "This isn't pure dirt. It's mixed with other building materials." It might infect him or cause medical complications, especially since the wound was located on his head—his head, which absolutely had to stay healthy so his thinking would remain clear and healthy. He said, "But this building is centuries old and during that time the building materials have mixed together, dissolved, and decomposed, leaving only dirt. Here they are returning to the earth from which they emerged, turning back to dirt."

He began to play with his hands, intertwining his fingers, separating them, and then joining them again. He spread out the palms of his hands and then pressed them together. He counted his fingers, finger by finger: little finger, ring finger, middle finger, index finger, and thumb. With the index finger of his right hand he traced the lines of his left palm. Then he reversed hands and performed the same operation. He extended his operations upward and passed his right palm over the entire length of his left arm, before changing arms. With both hands he investigated the other members of his body. He was fascinated by this sport and entranced by this game, the game of the body. Since he took so much delight in it, he removed his remaining garments and continued playing the game of the body. He imagined the structural elements and the distances, the ambiance of different areas and their magical congruities and symmetries. He felt the formations of the living body and its perfection. All this was revealed by creative touches, by the movement of his fingers and the palms of his hands. He became lost in his body's labyrinths, hunting for tidbits of information, probing deeply into its curves, cavities, and corners, tracking down its details, passing over elevations, plains, and valleys, from mountain peak to coast, from the top of his head to the hollows of the soles of his feet. On his journey of discovery he met sensitive regions. When he touched ticklish areas, he laughed. He stumbled upon an erect column, which lamented in that dark sky its continual longing for the eternal fountainhead. After that he explored his cavities, crossing the ravines. He probed his body with his ten fingers, touching it like a visionary, dreaming artist, discovering—for the first time in his life—the body's magic, splendor, vigor, beauty, and sanctity. He was overwhelmed by admiration for this body and felt respect and veneration for it. A creative, innovative force was evident in it. He leaned over his body to lick it with his tongue, curling himself into a ball, investigating every place he could reach, bowing humbly before his body to ask pardon and forgiveness from it, apologizing for all the pains he had caused it. He apologized on behalf of all those people whose ignorance and lack of appreciation of its value had caused it bruises and injuries. On behalf of all of them he raised the flag of liberation for the body.

"Yes, I'll raise the banner for its liberation. I'll wait until I emerge from this rock pile. I must emerge into the light to announce a revolution to liberate the body, carrying it even to the point of nudity. They have mistreated this body, denying it the respect and veneration it deserves."

He shouted as loudly as he could, "Thank you, Cave-In, for causing me to discover, at last, the secret of this body."

Then, feeling exhausted, he reclined on his back. Remembering the pain he had experienced in his left leg, he bent forward to examine it, but discovered no wound. He felt cold sting his extremities and move to the rest of his body but attributed no importance to this. He was overwhelmed by an extraordinary fatigue he could no longer withstand. So he stretched out on the ground and fell into a deep sleep. He dreamed he was walking aimlessly past an assembly point for caravans. He heard a herald proclaim the imminent departure of a caravan heading for the City of Light. This name awakened mysterious aches in him, and he felt an unruly urge to travel. His heart sank in his chest as his desire became ever more intense. The urge to travel raged through him.

He wanted to plunge headlong into a world he did not know and to leave behind this country, where they could wrangle to their hearts' delight. He would go off to observe what was happening there, in the City of Light.

He had read about this city in an old book he had stumbled upon one day while investigating his grandmother's secret caches. It had been slipped between other things at the bottom of an antique chest. The book's manuscript had been severely damaged by long neglect. Its pages were yellow, tattered, and worm-eaten, and their edges were flaking off like hair from a skull in an ancient tomb.

When he asked his grandmother about it, she listened to him attentively. Then she was silent for a long time as she tried to remember. Finally she told him, "It's a legacy from your grandfather, who wrote it himself with extraordinary care." She added, referring to the grandfather, "He was infatuated with travel and used to jot down in that book his observations and comments and the adventures he experienced during his difficult voyage."

So his desire to see the City of Light began when he first read the pages of the manuscript that his grandfather had left behind. When he heard that the caravan was setting out for this city, his troubled universe was enveloped in a miserable dark veil, and he felt a violent desire to travel with that caravan. A geographical cure is tempting when you are confronted by a world in which you can accomplish nothing.

He readied his food and his kit and, heaving his pack onto his back, gripped the stick of departure to seek the Creator who never disappoints those who seek Him. On his voyage he passed by dense thorny thickets, lofty frightening bare mountains, rocky paths, desolate deserts, heaving seas, and parched wastelands. After many difficulties and tribulations, as day broke one morning he came upon the City of Light and sighed deeply.

The moment he set foot in this city he had a bad feeling about it, for he found it teeming with a jumbled mixture of diverse forms of anarchy. Either the Master Craftsman's hand had never touched it or His touch had been long absent. It was a terrifying outlet for turmoil. In every nook were assembled marvels and wonders, but pains and refuse were stockpiled there as well. Thorns and dry weeds sprouted there, and brackish water collected in its depressions, which were inhabited by noxious pests and reptiles, along with blue larvae. Living amid its piles of rocks were several species of viper. At every moment, wild mad dogs prowled the streets. Cats clawed at each other, livestock roamed freely there, and foul odors filled the air.

Plague-ridden jerboas and rats naturally flourished on its soil, where they made dens from which to launch predatory raids. From it issued hosts of mosquitoes, flies, and exotic insects that rained stings on people's faces, releasing their venom and spreading diseases and plagues.

All the inhabitants of this city were blind. Their

beards were thick and black, and the hair of their heads hung down to their shoulders. They wore almost no clothes except for a band fastened around their genitals. The amazing thing about these blind people was that they moved about quickly and deftly. Each took his stick and investigated the surrounding area, just as if it were a pair of eyes.

When Murtada bumped into one of them, the man shouted at him, "Don't you have a stick to see what's in front of you?"

Another man quickly responded, "Perhaps he's still trying to feel things out with his eyes."

Terrified people on every side yelled, "There's a stranger among us from the City of Dark Clouds."

They immediately surrounded him and seized him firmly. They began to paw at him and touched his eyes with their sticks. When they discovered he could see, they told him, "The best thing for you is to become like us and see things with your stick."

They pressed fingers like screws, augers, and drills against his face to poke out his eyes. He began to scream for help, yelling in terror. Then he shook off his sleep and found he was screaming and trembling. When he opened his eyes, the world around him was black, and—in his fright—he thought he had gone blind. Gradually his alarm faded as he remembered that he was in a hole and that the house had collapsed on top of him. So his terror subsided and he calmed down, but it had certainly been a terrifying dream. He felt worried, deeming this dream an ill omen. This was an old habit that had probably become engrained in him over the years, for he had long consid-

ered ill-omened those frightening dreams that had afflicted him wherever he had gone, throughout all the
stages of his life.

He told himself, "Those dreams that you so frequently
considered ill-omened have today been fulfilled, because
what could be more atrocious than your present condition? Things cannot get any worse. So what are you afraid
of? Why are you worried about ill omens now? All your
exquisite dreams have come to pass."

He laughed sarcastically and continued: "It's time for
you to celebrate, Murtada. All your beautiful dreams have
been fulfilled. Here you are enjoying the darkness of the
sun, taking pleasure in the cold drafts of heaters, feasting
your eyes on the light of the tomb. You wash with dry rubble, eat hunger, drink thirst, wear nakedness, and live
death. What more could you request than this? You have
ascended to the depths. There will be no threat to your
life whatsoever as long as you remain ensconced on the
throne of the abyss, buried alive in the dark recesses of this
summit. What more wondrous fate could lie in wait for
you? You used to think that events like these you are experiencing only flourished in your dreams. Now they're
the reality confronting you."

He had more to say to himself. "At present, in the
depths of this hole, you are living a life stranger than that
you used to see in your dreams and much more bizarre
than anything your imagination cooked up. Your life has
been at risk for a long time. You were buried alive almost
every day. That happened without your being aware of it.
You struggled with life and fought it and thus were distracted from all the dangers that surrounded you. You

wrestled with despair, powerlessness, and ruination. You struggled and struggled and struggled.

"Now, what should you do? The devastation you feared and contested has occurred. You are sitting at the bottom of this hole, powerless and abject. What has happened just now? What has changed?"

He put his head in his hands and began to reflect. He told himself: "Once everything has been demolished, then everything begins anew. The important thing is that you're still alive. All that's happened is that you've migrated from one world to another.

"You've migrated to a world of silence and contemplation, leaving a world of spectacle and its denizens: people who compete and contend with each other and who employ deception, fraud, lies, and barren debates as their favored methods. Theirs is a world of specters, phantoms, and suspicions, destined to end at this, the appointed hour. You have journeyed by night from the silence of living creatures to the silence of contemplation, which is endless, extending through an eternal time that has no terminus.

"Only now do you feel that you've been liberated from all your loathsome burdens, from your trivial concerns, and from all those things that hampered your life and shackled you. You've been liberated from all your daily routines, from your responsibilities, appointments, and duties. You've been liberated from hours, days, and years. You've been freed from paperwork, cards, documents, and numbers. You've been liberated from the categories of impermissible and permissible, of illicit and licit, of this and of that: from everything.

"You have been liberated from everything except thought, which never pauses, never quiets down, and never rests. What an infernal gadget it is! Thought keeps right on working without growing tired or exhausted. It only becomes more refractory, stronger, and more inflated when the eye finds nothing to observe. It does not quit for a moment, whether a person is awake or asleep. No matter how hard you try to make it pause or cease, it never stops pursuing you. It grants you no respite.

"It seems to have nothing better to do than to probe the depths of your being ceaselessly. You wish you had a pen and paper and a bit of sunlight so that you could return to the beginning in order to write, now, what it dictates to you: 'Grasping his hand, she hurried through the Halfaouine neighborhood to Bab Souïka. From there she dragged him into the souks of the old city, through swelling crowds, past clamorous vendors, kaleidoscopic hues, and variegated displays and finery. Surrendering himself to that world of colors, people, and objects, the boy forgot the anxiety that had tormented him and relaxed his small hand, which had started to ache in the woman's firm grip. . . . ' Who can extinguish the flames of this war, which is raging inside my head and pulsing through my blood, and give me back Dar al-Basha?

"This is the disquieting puzzle: how time passes. What profound secret has drawn me back to you, causing me to sever all my ties to the world and to hasten back to throw myself before you? I told myself: I'll discover all over again your hidden trophies, the magic you conceal, the treasures you hide, and that wealth of legends and wonders. After suffering gripped me with an iron hand and then led me to you again in a flimsy, disheveled garment, my roots severed, like soft dough ready to be molded into any shape, I renounced the world and everything in it and turned my back on all its spurious attractions and whatever shimmered before me—on account of my failures and weakness. I felt such despair about myself that people feared for me. They said, 'You're a pale, mutilated replica of those congested areas in Dar al-Basha with their dilapidated, leaning walls, broken-down doorways, and cracked terraces from which dry grass sprouts beside swelling, cancerous tumors and other deep scars. Moreover, you are totally lacking in will, are absolutely incapable of coping, antisocial, unable to forge ties to other people or to focus your energies, weighed down by anxieties, suffering from crushing fear and ill health, extremely depressed and nervous, and so introverted that you seem a hedgehog. Besides that, you don't know the difference between profit and loss.'

"All this, because you could never expel the specter of Dar al-Basha from your memory and never let an hour go by without thinking of it. You never doubted for a moment your birthright to this neighborhood in which your grandfathers lived with all their strength and with every fiber of their being. The neighborhood may well show signs of old age, but allowing its landmarks and characteristic features to be obliterated would be inexcusable."

Murtada was so engrossed in his reflections that he reached this point without being conscious of the time they took or of passing hours or days. Indeed, he was no longer concerned about anything that occurred outside this cave. Now that the world was his to command, he soared through it, proceeding freely wherever he chose, completely independent of his body. He no longer felt hunger or thirst. He forgot all about his body as he changed into an abstract spirit that soared far away and into thought that operated without interruption, traveling at the speed of light and never stopping, traversing any length of time, freely and independently, as he set out through the thunderous silence.

He asked, "How has this come about? Now, then, Dar al-Basha! What an epoch separated me from you until the day I turned back to you! I doubt that you can count the ages or number them, no more than I can, even if I tried. This is even more fantastic than the *Thousand and One Nights*, but mine are mere ravings, the ravings of a lover.

"How strange you are, Dar al-Basha! You'll never be simply a stone carefully laid, walls, portals and windows, or a beautiful edifice. You're something much grander and more profound than that. You're far greater than the ruin into which you've fallen, greater than the painful blows of time. Because of your strong spirit, you'll endure through the ages."

He said again resolutely, "The important thing is for your spirit to remain strong, for your will to stay resolute, for your determination to be like iron, for you to know how to bind your wounds and to relieve your pain, like courageous knights and brave men, too. The important thing is for you to endure and for your will to remain like iron: there in the sunshine to wring gloom's neck and to defend your freedom.

"It makes no difference if your condition evolves, for that's a sign of health. Surely you lent an ear to the shaykh thoroughly versed in knowledge and in the disclosure of the hidden characteristics of things, the scholar Ibn Khaldun, when he declared within your precincts, 'Another source of error for the historian is overlooking change in the conditions of nations and generations over the course of changing eras and with the passing days. It is a serious malady that is hard to detect, since the symptoms manifest themselves only after long periods have elapsed. Hardly anyone notices it, except for an elite among mankind. The conditions of the world and of nations, with all their different customs and their sects, do not persist according to a single fashion and in a constant form. There is, rather, a fluctuation over time and through different eras and a transition from one condition to another, whether for individual people, times, or major cities. In just the same way, whole provinces, regions, ages, and states change over time.'[3] This holds true for Dar al-Basha as well."

Murtada plunged into a spinning, feverish whirlpool, where dreams became confused with observations from life and reality mixed with the world of the imagination. His ears began to reverberate with a thunderous roar. He could not tell whether it was the roar of silence or the roar

---

3. From an introductory statement for Ibn Khaldun's world history, rather than from the *Muqaddima*; see Ibn Khaldun, *Le Livre des Exemples*, trans. Abdesselam Cheddadi, 1:40. Ibn Khaldun, who was born in Tunis in 1332 and died in Cairo in 1406, was a renowned historian celebrated as one of the fathers of sociology for the *Muqaddima* or "Introduction" to his world history.

of engines and backhoes arriving to extract him from his pit.

The roar rocked his ears ever more violently and his ravings reached fever pitch. Suddenly a serene calm descended upon him. He was flooded by a brilliant light, which filled his heart. Happiness coming from an unknown source affected him, and he was filled with determination and hope. Summoning all his strength, he released a resounding yell that shook every pillar. Its echo reverberated to the farthest reaches of the world. He dealt the boulder confining him a single blow, shattering it into chips that flew in every direction. He rose, shaking the dust from himself.

How often have I been slain and perished, by your account,
Only to shake off the dust as tomb and shroud vanish.[4]

---

4. Abu al-Tayyib al-Mutanabbi, *Diwan al-Mutanabbi*. This couplet, from a poem by al-Mutanabbi (ca. 915–965), responds to a rumor at the court of Sayf al-Dawla that the poet had died. In the quotation in this novel, the couplet reads *"hum"* (or "their") instead of *"kum"* ("your").

18

Murtada al-Shamikh opened his eyes to discover he was stretched out in bed, under the cover . . . unharmed. Lifting his head from the pillow, he glanced around inquisitively. Everything was where it belonged. His world was right: walls, ceiling, doors, and windows; nothing had changed. Tossing the cover from his body, he leapt out of bed, rushed to the door, and pushed it wide open with a single thrust. Light swept through the room.

He stepped into the dwelling's expansive, welcoming courtyard where radiant sunshine flashed against the white walls. His brother's children—Amin, Samia, and Thuraya—were playing with their grandfather.

The furrows in Murtada's forehead relaxed and his face shone with astonished delight as he walked toward the children. He held his arms open wide for them, and they raced to him. After placing one on his shoulder and the other two under his wings, he soared across the courtyard. They protested merrily, hilariously, filling the world with a giddy splendor.

The family was gathered for breakfast. A variety of

tempting dishes had been prepared and their tantalizing aromas filled the air: freshly baked bread, crispy fried pancakes with cups of honey, and bowls filled with milk fresh from the farm.

> Everything was merely a dream:
> A dream within a dream,
> A dream arising from a dream,
> A dream emerging from a dream's womb,
> A dream that rested atop a dream.
> Dreams had been superimposed on one another,
> Till the interlacing and intertwining of dreams
> Challenged the imagination.

The family formed a harmonious whole, the grandfather occupying the center. His sons, daughters, and grandchildren were assembled around him, encircling him on every side, generating a happy, agitated clamor as their laughter resounded. It was a bright, beautiful morning.

Murtada gazed at them with a surging love and hurried eagerly to join their circle. Only now did he sense that his spirit, which had deserted him, was returning to seek refuge among them, to settle there in the folds of their embrace, to listen to the warmth of their voices, without ever ceasing to enjoy listening to them or growing bored.

He asked himself: Am I asleep or awake? How much longer will I be a prisoner of my dreams, imagining that I'm walking in my sleep, living reality in a dream and dreaming while awake? Will I always mistake dreams for tangible reality, responding—as if my nervous system were wired in reverse—to risible moments with a scream and to frightening events with delight? That happened in the past, whenever I made my way to Shama's house. When she hurried toward me, I would step aside. Then I would search for her face. Once I glimpsed her, I would stand there, struck dumb by her black eyes and milky mouth. She moved delicate fingers, plunging a needle into silk, embroidering her wedding dress, while launching a luminous smile as the scent of musk spread from her throughout the room. A bright moon . . . an open window . . . waiting. . . .

Who will restore my beautiful dreams to me?

Who will restore Shama to me?

Who will restore my lost childhood?

Works by Hassan Nasr

Bibliography

Works by
Hassan Nasr

Layali al-Matar (Rainy Nights). 1967. 2nd ed. Tunis: al-Dar al-Tunisiya li-l-Nashr, 1978. Short stories.

Dahaliz al-Layl (Night Passages). Tunis: Manshurat al-Jadid, 1977. Novel.

52 Layla (Fifty-Two Nights). Tunis: Manshurat al-Jadid, 1979. Short stories.

Khubz al-Ard (Our Daily Bread). Tunis: al-Dar al-Tunisiyah li-l-Nashr, 1985. Novel.

Sahar wa-l-Jurh (Insomnia and the Wound). Tunis: al-Dar al-Tunisiyah li-l-Nashr, 1989. Short stories.

Dar al-Basha (The Pasha's Residence). Tunis: Dar al-Jadid li-l-Nashr, 1994. Novel.

Khuyul al-Fajr (Dawn Mares, or Pipedreams). Tunis: Dar al-Yamama li-l-Nashr wa-l-Tawzia', 1997. Short stories.

Sijillat Ra's al-Dik (Cockhead's Files). Tunis: Cérès Éditions, 2001. Novel.

Bibliography

Attar, Farid ud-Din. *The Conference of the Birds*. Translated by Afkham Darbandi and Dick Davis. Harmondsworth: Penguin Books, 1984.

Fanon, Frantz. *Toward the African Revolution*. Trans. Haakon Chevalier. New York: Grove Press, 1967.

———. *The Wretched of the Earth*. Trans. Constance Farrington. New York: Grove Press, 1966.

Fontaine, Jean. *Le Roman tunisien de langue arabe, 1956–2001*. Tunis: Cérès Éditions, 2002.

Hawi, Khalil. *Nahr al-Ramad*. 3rd printing. Beirut: Dar al-Tali'a li-l-Tiba'a wa-l-Nashr, 1963.

Ibn Hisham, Abd Allah Ibn Yusuf. *Qatr al-Nada wa-Ball al-Sada*. Edited by Muhammad Abd al-Mun'im Khaffaji et al. Cairo: Dar al-Kitab al-Misri and Beirut: Dar al-Kitab al-Lubnani, 1992.

Ibn Khaldun. *Le Livre des Exemples*. Vol. 1. Translated by Abdesselam Cheddadi. Paris: Gallimard, 2002.

Ibn Malik. *Alfiya Ibn Malik*. Edited by Al-Hajj Musa Ibn Muhammad al-Daghistani. Cairo: Maktabat al-Adab, 1984.

Marra, Michele. *Modern Japanese Aesthetics: A Reader*. Honolulu: University of Hawaii Press, 1999.

Memmi, Albert. *The Colonizer and the Colonized*. New York: Orion, 1965.

al-Mutanabbi, Abu al-Tayyib. *Diwan al-Mutanabbi*. 1923. Reprint, Cairo: al-Markaz al-Arabi li-l-Bahth wa-l-Nashr, 1980.

———. *Diwan Shaykh Shua'ara' al-'Arabiya*. Edited by 'Abd al-Mun'im Khaffaji et al. Cairo: Maktaba Misr, 1994.

al-Shabbi, Abu al-Qasim. *Aghani al-Hayat*. Tunis: al-Dar al-Tunisiya li-l-Nashr, 1966.

al-Shanfara. *Lamiyat al-Arab*. Edited by Abd al-Halim Hifni. Cairo: Maktabat al-Adab, 1981.

al-Shibli, Abu Bakr. *Diwan Abi Bakr al-Shibli*. Edited by Muwaffaq Fawzi al-Jabr. Damascus: Dar Batra li-l-Nashr wa-Tawzi', 1999.